Secrets...hopes...dreams...

Welcome to

*Silver

*Spires

where

School Friends

are

forever!

D1367563

Collect the *School Friends* series:

Welcome to Silver Spires
Drama at Silver Spires
Rivalry at Silver Spires
Princess at Silver Spires
Secrets at Silver Spires
Star of Silver Spires

Princess
at
Silver Spires

Ann Bryant

USBORNE

My thanks to Celia Pollington and Amy Hodgson
for their invaluable help with this book

First published in the UK in 2008 by Usborne Publishing Ltd.,
Usborne House, 83-85 Saffron Hill, London EC1N 8RT, England.
www.usborne.com

Series cover design by Sally Griffin
Cover illustration by Suzanne Sales/New Division

The name Usborne and the devices ♀ 🎈 are Trade Marks of
Usborne Publishing Ltd.

A CIP catalogue record for this book is available from the British Library.

First published in America in 2013 AE.
PB ISBN 9780794531522   ALB ISBN 9781601303011
JFMAMJJ SOND/12   01566/2
Printed in Dongguan, Guangdong, China.

Chapter One

It's so peaceful here in the secret garden. I can sit on this bench and just think my own thoughts in silence. Not that I don't love the busy, buzzy side of boarding-school life, hanging out with my close friends in our dormitory, or at lunch, or racing around the track. But out of the six of us I think I'm the one who most needs to be alone sometimes. I came across the garden last September when I'd first started at this school. My best friend, Katy, found out about it too, and then a little later we told our other close friends where it was. It's tucked away behind a high hedge way on the other side of the athletics field and we six from Amethyst dorm think we're still the only ones who know about it.

The school is called Silver Spires, and it's the best boarding school in the world. On a day like today, when the sun shines on the main building's tall spires, they really seem to sparkle like silver. It gives me a nice warm feeling, seeing them reaching into the sky, and I love the thought that this is the same sun that shines onto my home country in Africa.

I come from Ghana, and I'm a princess, but I absolutely hate people knowing that. I tried like crazy to keep it a secret when I first came here, but in no time at all people found out, and it was exactly as I'd feared. Lots of girls suddenly wanted to be my friend, not because they liked me but because they liked the idea of having a princess for a friend. But, worse than that, the ones who didn't rush to be my best friend went around saying I was stuck-up and that I thought I was something special. I was miserable for a while and it was Katy who came to my rescue. At her old school everyone had wanted to be her friend too, because they knew that her mom is a famous actress. But that's one secret that will never *ever* come out here at Silver Spires. Katy only told me about it at first, but then before fall break she told the others too. I'll never forget that moment. We were all sitting in a circle on the rug in our dorm and when Katy actually said her mother's real name you could have heard the sun rising. But the six of us best friends from Amethyst dorm are sworn to secrecy about that now.

The glinting sun in this warm spring air is like a dim reminder of the bright sun that bakes the earth of Ghana, and I can't stop my thoughts from slipping away to all the poor people I saw last week during spring break, when I went with my family to visit our home country. It made me sad and upset when I met a girl named Abina and saw with my own eyes what she has to do every day. She's twelve years old, the same age as me, and at five o'clock each morning she goes to a muddy waterhole, where animals drink, to collect water for her family. It takes hours for the water to seep through the ground and for the mud to settle, and even then it's dirty and not safe to drink. But I visited other villages in north Ghana where a charity called Just Water has built wells and installed hand pumps, so the people there can have clean water.

My father is the president of Just Water and now I've started to help the charity too. I'm really pleased to do this work because I feel so lucky to have the life I have, when there are so many people in northern Ghana who don't even survive to my age. How can that be fair? I repeat this question over and over like a mantra to myself, when I'm out here alone in the fresh spring air. But I never come up with any answers, just resolutions never to forget the people of Ghana.

Sitting here on my bench, I shivered as I looked at my watch, and got a shock because it was six thirty. I only had a few minutes to shake off African Princess Naomi and get myself back into regular-sixth-grade-Silver-Spires Naomi, having dinner with her friends. Well, to tell the truth I never completely shake the princess part of me away, but I always try my best to keep it well hidden.

As I got closer to our boarding house, Hazeldean, I saw Katy standing outside, her shoulders hunched up and her arms folded tightly. She waved when she saw me and came running over.

I hugged her. "You look frozen, Kates!"

"So do you!"

We laughed and I realized she was right. "I've been wrapped up in my thoughts in the secret garden, but I can't say they kept out the cold very well!"

"I guessed you'd be there," said Katy, looking suddenly serious. "Are you okay?"

I knew why she was asking me that. She'd listened

in complete silence yesterday evening when I'd told her all about my time in Ghana, and at the end she'd said she felt guilty that I'd spent my spring break working for a charity while she'd been having a great time in LA with her mom. "You make me feel really spoiled, Naomi," were her precise words. But I'd quickly told her not to be silly, because Katy and her mom are so close and don't get to spend much time together, and anyway, I felt ten times more spoiled than that when I saw Abina's school – which was scarcely more than a tree and a wooden hut – and I compared it with Silver Spires.

"I can't stop thinking about Abina," I told her quietly, as we walked across to the cafeteria, which is in the main building.

"You can't do any more than you're doing, working for Just Water," Katy said, linking arms with me.

Maybe she was right, but it didn't stop a little niggling voice telling me I must do more.

"Slow down, you two!" came Georgie's urgent cry from way behind. Katy and I turned around to see her half walking, half jogging, as though she was on her last legs at the end of a torturous marathon. "Why do people move so fast around here?"

I couldn't help smiling as we waited for her to

catch up to us. Georgie is always so dramatic, but in a great way.

"I lost track of the time watching my *Ugly Betty* DVD," she informed us in her puffed-out voice, when she finally drew level. "It's totally cool. You should see it. I'm starving now, though. What's on the menu, do you know?"

"No clue," said Katy, as I slipped back into my other world for a moment, thinking about poverty and starvation. But I quickly shook the thoughts away. I knew they didn't do anyone any good.

Georgie's best friend, Mia, was in the line for food, and beckoned to us all to join her, but I didn't think it was fair for the three of us to cut in like that, so just Georgie went ahead. A moment later she was right back, full of something she was dying to tell us. "Mia says that one of the tenth graders has been looking for you, Naomi!"

I frowned and wondered what that was about. "Did Mia say who?"

"Someone named Elise. I think she's that one with the hair like Rachel from *Friends*, but Mia said she couldn't really remember what her hair was like, just that she seemed a bit put out that you weren't around, and even more put out when Mia said she had no idea where you were." Georgie winked at us and added, "Yeah, right!" All my friends knew that if I wasn't around then I was probably in the secret garden, and they'd never let on about it. Then she looked thoughtful. "Actually I don't think it *could* have been Elise, because she's got a reputation for never deigning to speak to anyone below ninth grade!"

A few minutes later I was sitting at a table with Katy, Georgie and Mia, listening to Georgie questioning Mia on what "the girl" looked like.

"You're so funny, Georgie!" said Mia. "Totally desperate to know, when Naomi's not particularly bothered."

Georgie didn't seem to hear her. "The thing is, if it *was* Elise, it must have been something pretty important." She was getting impatient. "Come on, guys, what do you think?"

I shrugged and changed the subject, because I'd suddenly realized I hadn't seen Grace and Jess since the last class. "Where are the other two?"

"There!" said Georgie, nodding toward the door and looking quite impressed with herself, as though she'd personally magicked them up for my pleasure.

I grinned at her, and Katy and I squished up on the bench to make room for them.

"One of the tenth graders was looking for you," said Grace, as she sat down.

"Whoa! Sounding urgent now! *Quelle intrigue!*" said Georgie, putting on a French accent.

"Who was it?" Katy asked.

"A girl named Elise," Grace replied.

Georgie gasped. "That one who looks like Rachel from *Friends*?"

Grace wrinkled her nose. "Um…does she?" Grace is the least into looks and fashion out of all of us. Her passion is sports, and when she's not in her school uniform she's in her tracksuit.

It was Jess who answered Georgie's question. "Yes, she's got streaky blonde hair and always wears a big barrette holding half of it back. And she's got a long neck and wide shoulders, and wears quite a bit of makeup," she added, which made us all laugh, it was such unexpected detail.

"What's funny about that?" asked Jess.

"Nothing!" said Grace, sticking up for her best friend. "We're all just jealous of your artist's eye that picks up every little thing."

"Did she say what she wanted?" asked Katy.

"It was right after school when we saw her and she didn't seem too pleased that she might have to wait until dinner before she saw Naomi," Grace said.

Then she lowered her voice as she turned to me. "Don't worry, we didn't tell her where she could find you."

"Even though I imagine she would have paid us for the info," Jess added. "She looked so…so anxious to get hold of you."

"Wow!" said Georgie. "I'd better be there when she *does* track you down!"

"Looks like your wish has come true," said Mia quietly.

We all followed her gaze and saw a much older student marching purposefully in our direction.

"That's her!" hissed Georgie. "That's Elise!"

I don't know why, but I suddenly felt uneasy. I hate being the center of attention and I found myself crossing my fingers that everyone was mistaken, and Elise wanted to speak to someone else. Anyone but me.

She squatted down in between Georgie and me, and Georgie immediately swizzled around a bit and leaned forward. The others were all silent too, as though waiting for a show to begin.

Elise blinked and I saw how thick her mascara was. She looked annoyed about everyone tuning in. "Uh…when you've finished, Naomi, I'd like a word," she said.

I wanted to get whatever it was over with, so I started to get up. "I'm finished *now*."

"Are you sure?" She was eyeing my half-eaten cheesecake, but there was no way I could manage it. I was just too nervous.

I followed her out of the cafeteria, certain the others were all staring after me, and as soon as we were in the hallway she turned into an empty classroom and shut the door. She perched on a desk while I stood opposite her. Now I was really nervous. Her face was so serious I began to wonder if I'd done something terribly wrong and was about to get a big telling-off.

"Naomi..." She suddenly broke into a huge smile, then leaned forward and grabbed both my wrists dramatically. "I've got something to ask you. I know you're going to find it totally unusual and you might wonder if I've got a screw loose or something, but believe me, I *do* know what I'm doing." She nodded slowly and paused, her eyes sparkling as she looked straight into mine. "I'd like *you*..." Another pause. I wished she'd just finish her sentence. "...to be one of my two models for the fashion show before the Easter vacation!"

I didn't understand what she meant. Katy is totally into fashion and wants to be a designer when she's older, so I did know that there was going to be a fashion show. But I was certain Katy had said it was for fashion design students, because I could remember her saying she couldn't wait until she was in ninth grade so she could take part. Then I suddenly had a thought. Maybe Elise had somehow heard about the incredible hip wraps and bracelets that Katy made for all of us just before spring break for Chinese New Year, and she thought I was the one who'd done them.

"Oh, I think you might be confusing me with Katy. She's a fantastic designer."

Elise's eyes shot wide open and she dropped my wrists as dramatically as she had grabbed them. "It's nothing to do with design. *I'm* the designer. I'm saying I want you to model for me." She suddenly frowned. "You *are* Naomi Okanta, aren't you?"

I felt myself tensing up, but I wasn't sure why.

"Yes," I replied, a bit abruptly.

She looked startled and I suddenly felt like an impertinent little girl talking back to a teacher, even though she was only a tenth grader. I think I must have sounded really rude. "But...I'm only in sixth grade..."

She suddenly smiled at me as though I was a little too young to get the hang of things, and then she spoke slowly and deliberately. "Okay, Naomi, the fashion show is for the students taking fashion design this year, and yes, it's true that most of them have chosen their models from ninth and tenth grade. But..." She opened her eyes wide, then broke into an even bigger smile. "...there's nothing in the rules to say that you can't have a model from any year! And let's get one thing straight, I *didn't* choose you because you're a princess. No way."

I still felt uncomfortable though. What other reason could there be for choosing a sixth grader, except that I was pretty tall? And if she particularly wanted a black model, there were plenty of other black girls in the older grades.

"I...I don't get why you want me...?"

She tipped her head to the side and smiled even more. "Because you've got the most wonderful posture. You stand so straight and walk so smoothly. You're tall and slim and elegant..." She giggled. "Need I say more?"

I couldn't help feeling flattered by what Elise had said, but I still thought there were plenty of other girls who could do it better than me.

"I'm not sure..."

I thought I saw a tiny flash of annoyance cross her face. Maybe I should be jumping at the chance.

I knew Katy would. But that's only because fashion is totally Katy's scene. Georgie would grasp the opportunity with both hands too, because she absolutely loves performing. I think the others would probably be like me, though – a little scared of the unknown.

Elise paused thoughtfully before she said her next words. "It's a big charity event, you know, Naomi."

My ears pricked up. "Oh, I didn't realize that. What charity is it?"

"Um...it's not completely been decided yet. I told Miss Owen – she's the fashion design teacher who's in charge of the whole thing – that I thought it should be a Third World charity."

I found myself getting really interested now, as a picture of Abina flashed through my mind. "So when will it be decided?"

Elise was looking at me carefully. "Well, the thing is, Miss Owen is open to suggestions. Do you...have a preference?"

"Yes, Just Water for Ghana!" I blurted out. "That's an amazing charity. Only forty-four percent of—"

"Okay! Just Water...right..." Elise jumped up. "I'll suggest it to Miss Owen. She's been asking for specific ideas." She touched my arm. "So...are you saying yes to being my number one model?"

"I...I..." My head was swimming with doubts. I hate being the center of attention. And I'd be terrified being the only sixth grader among a bunch of ninth and tenth graders. But if I could do anything to help Just Water, then I should.

Elise must have seen the struggle I was having. "Don't worry, Naomi. Think about it for a couple of days and I'll talk to Miss Owen about whether we can choose your charity...what was it? Just Water?"

I nodded.

"I'll get her to look it up on the internet. Then I'll come and find you tomorrow and you can tell me what you've decided, all right?"

I nodded weakly and she was gone like a whirlwind, leaving me in a strange daze, still flattered to have been asked and excited at the thought that I might be able to do something for my beloved charity, but confused and uneasy, and not really sure why.

Chapter Two

"How come I'm the only one who thinks Naomi's totally nuts?" Georgie was looking around at us with big staring eyes, her palms up, her mouth slightly open.

It was the next day and we were sitting in a circle on the round rug in the middle of our dorm. Katy had called a friendship meeting to discuss my dilemma. She already knew my worries, but felt that the others ought to have a say because she was, as she put it, "totally biased about anything to do with fashion."

"You're not the only one who thinks Naomi should

go for it," she told Georgie now. "But I definitely don't think you're nuts," she added, turning to me. Then a second later she was looking back at Georgie. "The thing is, Naomi's not like you..."

"That's right, I'm not...an actress, like you," I told her quietly. "I can't think of anything worse than having a whole audience watching me strut down a catwalk."

"Ooooh, it'd be sooooo cool!" squeaked Georgie, jumping up. Then she gave us a fantastic impression of a supermodel walking down the catwalk. In no time at all we were rocking with laughter, because Amethyst dorm isn't exactly designed for modeling, so Georgie could only take about two steps before she had to swing dramatically around. She finished by climbing the ladder to her bed and lying on her side with her leg in the air. "Da daa!" Then she changed to a booming announcer's voice. "Thank you, Georgie Henderson!" And we all broke into loud applause and whoops and cheers.

"Yes, thanks, Georgie!" said Mia, grinning at her. "But I'm not sure you're doing anything to help poor Naomi, you know!"

"Well actually," I admitted, "your demonstration helped a lot, Georgie, because you've made me realize I could never do it in a million years."

"Yes, you could!" said Katy. "I bet you'd be a natural!" She gave me an imploring look like a little child begging its mother for something. "Please, please say you'll do it, because then I can come along to fittings and rehearsals and learn first-hand about fabrics and design and everything. Please, please, pretty please." She suddenly stopped and looked apologetic. "Sorry, I'm just being selfish, aren't I? Forget everything I just said...except the part about you being a natural."

I gave her a grateful look but didn't say anything.

"I'm not sure I'd do it," said Jess thoughtfully, "because you're kind of stuck with wearing whatever they produce for you, aren't you?" Then she grinned. "But I guess there's no danger of anyone asking me anyway!"

"But what if you had to wear a bikini or something?" said Grace, clapping her hand over her mouth in horror. "I'd die!"

Mia covered her eyes, which made Georgie laugh. "Me too!"

"I can't imagine anyone designing a bikini," said Katy. "What normally happens is that you get categories like daywear, evening wear, and that kind of thing."

"Swimwear!" added Georgie, jumping down from her bed.

"I wish I'd asked Elise more questions now," I said, feeling myself cringing at the whole idea again and imagining how awful it would be if I had to wear something really short and tight, because that's not the sort of thing I feel comfortable in at all. In fact, I don't like any kind of dressing up, even when I have to wear formal traditional African outfits for photo shoots or public appearances with my family. It could actually be just my parents dressed up like that, and I still feel a little awkward with everyone staring at them. On my first day at Silver Spires, I wanted to sink through the ground when they dressed traditionally just to drop me off. If it was up to me, I'd wear jeans and a T-shirt all the time.

I knew I shouldn't get hung up about what I might have to wear for the fashion show and I scolded myself for being pathetic about doing something that could help a charity – and hopefully *my* charity. All I had to do was get some courage together.

"From what you said, Elise sounds pretty laid-back about it, giving you time to think and everything," said Katy. "Do you want me to talk to her to find out exactly what you'd have to wear?"

Immediately I felt worked up again, and wondered

what it was about what Katy had just said that was so scary. In the end I went to the secret garden and sat alone, staring at the silver spires, deep in thought. There wasn't any sun today and the spires looked steely gray and forlorn, poking into the overcast sky.

Katy thought Elise was laid-back, but when I pictured her talking to me the day before, grabbing my wrists and looking at me so intently, she seemed far from laid-back to me. But maybe that's how she was with everyone. And anyway, what did it matter if she was a little intense? I suppose famous designers must be like that too.

My thoughts soon turned to Ghana and I found myself going over everything I'd done at spring break. I think the worst experience was seeing a man with a horrible painful disease called Guinea worm, which you get by drinking unclean water. I pulled my feet up on the bench and hugged my knees, trying not to cry as I thought about his pain.

Okay. My decision was made. I didn't need to know any more about the fashion show. I just had to be sure that Miss Owen had definitely agreed to all the funds going to Just Water. As long as she did, I would do whatever Elise wanted me to do. It was a small price to pay if it meant Just Water could get more money.

* * *

The others had been very excited when I told them what I'd decided, especially Katy.

"Oh Naomi, that's fantastic! I can't wait! Make sure you tell Elise that you'll only model for her on condition that your best friend can come along whenever she wants!"

Mia put her arm around me. "See, you're doing two good things – one helping out your charity, and two, helping out your best friend!"

We stayed awake chatting until late but I didn't feel at all tired the next morning, just nervous about talking to Elise. She came to find me in the lunch line and this time she didn't suggest we went off on our own.

"So I talked to Miss Owen, Naomi, and she's totally fine with giving the money to your water charity thingy, so there you go!"

I had to be absolutely sure. "You actually said Just Water in Ghana?"

"Yes, you can check yourself if you want, but she was thrilled that I'd come up with something specific, and when I told her the idea had come from you, she was even more thrilled!"

Katy was squeezing my hand excitedly and

Georgie had turned around in front of me, waiting for me to reply.

"Okay, I'll do it," I said simply.

"Yea!" said Georgie.

"That's great!" said Elise. She sounded much calmer than she had the last time we'd talked, almost as though she'd had every confidence that I'd agree in the end. "If you come along to the fashion design room after lunch I can tell you more about it and show you how the outfits are shaping up."

I suddenly realized my hand was hurting because Katy was squeezing it so hard. "Oh yes, sorry...is it okay for Katy to come with me? She's really into fashion design and—"

Elise hardly glanced at Katy. "Yeah, fine. See you later then."

And she was off in another of her whirlwind exits, leaving the most beautiful smell of perfume hanging around us.

"Mmmm!" said Georgie, sniffing the air. "Gorgeous!"

Katy and I opened the door to the fashion design room to be met by a sudden blast of heavy music and loud talking and laughing. Around three of the walls were tables with lots of sewing machines on them. Only one of them was in use. In the middle of the room there was a block of six tables. Two girls were cutting out material there, with quite a few other girls standing around, watching and chatting. Then there were more girls hanging around a full-length mirror. I felt Katy tense up beside me, but I knew it was the excited kind of tension.

"I think I've died and gone to heaven!" she whispered as she stared around her.

"There's Elise," I said, feeling relieved to have spotted her near the mirror. Now at least I could look as though I knew what I was doing in tenth grade territory. I set off striding across the room, but instinctively I knew that Katy wasn't following me and, turning around, I saw I was right. She'd gone to talk to the girl on the sewing machine.

"Hiya!" said Elise, spotting me in the mirror. "Come with me!" She took my hand and pulled me over to a mannequin that had no head or legs, but was covered in shiny gold material. "This is called a tailor's dummy," she explained. "And this is the top of one of your outfits!"

I eyed the dummy warily, thinking that my body wasn't quite the same shape.

"Don't worry, it's just to give me an idea," said Elise. Then she grabbed a tape measure off a nearby table and said, "Let me do a quick measure up, actually."

I felt a little embarrassed because I had to take my sweatshirt off before she drew the tape around my chest, then my waist, and lastly my hips.

"Perfect!" she announced when she'd scribbled the figures down. "The skirt part of the dress is going to be short and tight and silver, and it'll be sequined and braided all the way up, to make an utterly fabulous little evening dress especially for *you*!"

Immediately I felt myself tensing up. I was going to have to wear the very thing I knew I'd absolutely hate wearing. Maybe I could ask Elise for something different. No, that was a ridiculous thought. She wouldn't change her designs just for me, would she? I didn't know what to say. This was a whole new world, so it was a relief when Katy suddenly appeared at my side.

"Satin, nice!" she said, rubbing the gold material between her finger and thumb. "Are there certain categories that you have to design for, Elise?"

"Yep, three," said Elise, getting me to turn around slowly while she looked at me, which was really embarrassing.

"Um...how many outfits will I actually be modeling on the day?" I stammered, trying to say something sensible.

Elise spoke lightly. "Only three. One from each category. So no big deal."

I sighed with relief.

Elise started to count them off on her fingers. "Yes, the first category is 'Dress to Impress for Less'. The second is—"

"I like the sound of that one," I interrupted, feeling silly the moment the words were out of my mouth, but went on anyway. "Katy does that kind of thing all the time, don't you, Kates?"

Elise ignored me completely and continued. "The second one is 'Caj with a Dash', which is just a quirky way of saying 'fashionable but casual'. It's not exactly a perfect rhyme, is it, but who cares? Miss Clemence thought of that one and she's French so..." Elise didn't finish her sentence.

"Yes, I know. She's *our* French teacher," said Katy. "And she does junior fashion club as well. 'Caj with a Dash', that sounds cool." Katy's eyes danced with excitement as she turned to me. "You'll look gorgeous, Naomi." Then she swung back to Elise. "Will the fashion show be videoed?"

Elise looked at her as though she'd just asked

whether Africa was bigger than England. "Obviously," she said, with a little sneer. "There'll be the official DVD for all the parents, but the local press will be there too, and this year they're even featuring it on the local TV news."

"Oh wow!" Katy said, while I swallowed and felt a new wave of nervousness coming over me at the thought of people being able to watch the fashion show not just once, but as often as they liked on the DVD.

"Oh, and Naomi," Elise added, "be prepared to be interviewed, with you being...so into the charity."

I gulped. I hadn't thought about being interviewed on TV, but I'd have to be brave and just get on with it, because it would be good publicity for Just Water. I'd done interviews before, for magazines and things, so hopefully it wouldn't be too terrifying. I told myself I'd cross that bridge when I came to it anyway. For the moment, I still wanted to know more basic facts, like exactly how many times I'd have to walk up and down the catwalk.

"And the third category," Elise went on, "is my personal fave – the 'Prom' category."

"Prom?"

"Surely you know what a prom dress is!"

"No, I..."

"It's a totally glam evening dress for a prom party."

"A prom party?"

"Oh dear," said Elise when she saw my puzzled face. "You *have* got a lot to learn. Prom parties are what us tenth graders like to do..." She laughed. "School time, holiday time, any time! Hence this creation here!" She waved her hand at the material on the dummy, then spotted someone across the room. "Oh, here comes Tansy."

A girl who was only slightly taller than me but quite a bit bigger was strolling over toward us. She had the straightest blonde hair I'd ever seen, a really pale complexion, and a rather sulky expression on her face.

"Tansy, this is Naomi, the one I told you about."

Tansy looked me up and down and gave me a half smile, as though she couldn't really be bothered to stretch her mouth any wider. "Hi." Then she turned back to Elise. "Made any decisions about the shoes? Because I'm going shopping this weekend and I'll get them then."

Elise looked mysterious. "Yes, I have! I'll tell you later. And I think I'll come on the shopping trip with you, but let's get a taxi, okay? Then we won't waste any time waiting for buses."

"Yeah, whatever."

"Tansy's my other model, by the way, Naomi. She's used to wearing expensive clothes, like you are."

"Well actually, I'm not used to dresses like—"

"There are fifteen of us designers and we're only allowed two models each, so we have to design and make six outfits. And we've all chosen models that we think will suit our designs."

"Not that the models are being judged, of course," said Tansy, frowning at her nails.

Something like an electric shock shot through my body. "Judged! I didn't know it was a competition…"

I caught a look that passed quick as a flash between Elise and Tansy, but a second later Elise was smiling a laid-back smile, her hand on my shoulder. "No, you've got the wrong idea here, Naomi. It isn't a competition. No, Tansy wasn't speaking literally. She was just saying, you know…"

"Everyone's more interested in the clothes than the models," Tansy finished off.

"Yeah, that's right," said Elise. She pulled her barrette out, then scooped back her tumbling hair into a rough bun and stuck the barrette back in. "Anyway, I'd better get back to work. I'll let you know when there's something for you to try on."

I felt as though Katy and I were being dismissed. "Um…is it okay for me to come along another time?" Katy asked.

Elise shrugged. "As long as you're not bothering anyone, I guess that's fine."

Katy thanked her and we went toward the door, only slowing down to look at what the girl on the sewing machine was doing. "Her name is Lara," whispered Katy as we approached her. "I talked to her when you were with Elise. She's so skillful!"

"Sorry, I was in a zone there!" Lara said, when she looked up and saw us watching her. She rubbed the back of her neck. "I wish I didn't get neck ache all the time! I must not be sitting right." Then she looked more carefully at me. "You've got a beautifully straight back. Elise is lucky to have you modeling for her. Congratulations, by the way! You're the youngest model by far."

"I'm a little nervous about that."

"Don't worry, you'll be fine." Lara smiled a really warm smile, then her face clouded over with concentration as she went back to work, and Katy and I crept out.

"It's so buzzy and exciting in there, isn't it?" said Katy, her eyes bright.

I nodded, not really feeling quite so convinced

as Katy about that. "Thank goodness it's not a competition, Kates. I nearly had a heart attack when Tansy said something about being judged, but then I felt stupid because I'd misunderstood what she meant."

Katy put her arm around me. "You'll soon get used to everything, Naomi."

"Lara's nice, isn't she?" I said, trying to find something positive to say.

"Yes, she's sweet. I'm not so sure about Elise though." Katy wrinkled her nose. "She made me feel about six and a half."

"I know what you mean. And I didn't really like Tansy either." I sighed, going over all that had just happened in the design room in my head, but then I came out of my daydream because we were just passing two sixth grade girls named Penny and Ali. Penny was from the same house as us, Hazeldean, but Ali was from Elmhurst. They seemed to be looking at me in a strange way. A moment later, when we'd gone around the corner to join the path that led back to Hazeldean, Katy stopped to get a stone out of her shoe, and I felt my stomach tighten when I heard Penny say, "She's modeling at the senior fashion show. She must think she is something else."

Then Ali put on a really stuck-up voice. "Look at me! Look at me! I'm a model princess!"

In a flash Katy straightened up and put her arm around my shoulder again. "Just ignore them. They're stupid!" she hissed.

But I couldn't ignore the wave of misery that welled up inside me.

Chapter Three

At Silver Spires we have clubs or free time after classes finish, then dinner, and lastly study hour, which is like homework except that we all sit in silence in a large room in our boarding house. In Hazeldean we're supervised by Miss Carol, or Miss Fosbrook, or occasionally Miss Jennings, the dorm mom. And from eight thirty, when study hour finishes, we're free until bedtime at nine, though we're not allowed to leave the boarding house during that half-hour. We often use this time to e-mail or call our parents, and tonight I really wanted to talk to mine. Well, to be precise, I wanted to talk to my dad.

Katy and I have a lot in common, but the one thing that's totally different between us is our relationship with our parents. I envy her being so close to her mom and dad and knowing that she can completely relax when she's with them. I've been brought up in a very different way. I lived the first part of my life in Ghana with my two older sisters and my little brother, and we had a huge house and servants to do everything. My brother and sisters and I didn't see much of our parents because we were always with our nannies, and whenever we did see them we had to be extremely polite and respectful.

Starting at a prep school in America two years ago seemed like a massive upheaval after living in Africa. The boys at the school kept their distance and the girls crowded around me as though I was an interesting rare specimen at a museum. *Princessus Africanus.* I didn't say much because I found it hard to adjust to my new life, but then as I settled in and began to talk more, the girls grew over-the-top friendly, suddenly wanting me to come to dinner with them and inviting themselves back to my house. I think they were expecting our house to be like the White House, which it definitely isn't. It's true that it is pretty big, because there are four floors, but some of the students lived in houses out in the country with lots of land and pastures, whereas we have hardly any land.

I still don't see my parents very much, and obviously even less since I've been at Silver Spires, and it's also true that they still have a small staff working for them. But they don't sit on thrones and the floors aren't made of gold, as some of my prep school friends believed.

Even though I don't have the same kind of closeness with my parents as Katy has with her mom, I'm getting closer and closer to my dad. He's such a wise man and I really needed his advice this evening. I'd been getting myself into more and more of a state about the fashion show, because I absolutely couldn't bear the thought that people might think I'm a big show-off, wearing all those glamorous clothes and strutting along a catwalk with lots of girls who are way older than me. Then last night, when I couldn't get to sleep for worrying about it, I actually thought about pulling out of the whole thing. After all, I wouldn't be letting the charity down, because it's definitely been decided to donate the money raised to Just Water. All I wanted was to hear my dad agreeing with me, and then I'd somehow feel stronger about breaking the news to Elise.

While I was listening to the phone ringing, I was

trying to imagine whereabouts in the house Dad might be, and what he might be doing. Probably working in his office. As it happened, it was one of the housekeepers who answered, and she went right off to find him.

"Naomi..." came his voice a minute later.

"Hello, Dad. How are you and Mom?"

"Both very well, my dear. And you?"

"I'm fine, but there's something I wanted to talk to you about..."

"Yes, of course."

"Well, you see, there's a fashion show in a few weeks and one of the older girls has asked me to model for her, even though I'm only a sixth grader and all the other models are lots older, and—"

"Modeling in a fashion show? That sounds very glamorous!"

"Yes, it does, doesn't it?"

I paused, waiting for Dad to go on and say that "glamorous" was not at all appropriate, and then insist that I pulled out, which would be perfect. But he didn't say anything at all, so I had to go on. "The thing is, I don't really want to be a model, but the money from the tickets is going to Just Water. That was...my idea."

"That's great news, Naomi! I'm proud of you for

that. And Mom will be proud too. It's wonderful that Just Water will benefit from the show. And if I remember rightly from the school calendar, parents are invited, so we'll come and support it, of course."

I instantly tensed up, partly because Dad wasn't saying the things I'd been hoping he'd say, and partly because a picture of my parents wearing their African finery and rolling up in one of their chauffeur-driven limousines was flashing through my mind. They don't understand how badly I want to blend in with all the other students here. In fact it was their limousine, even before their clothes, that attracted attention when I very first arrived at Silver Spires.

A feeling of urgency for Dad to understand my predicament was welling up inside me. "The horrible thing about the fashion show, Dad, is that now people in my grade know I'm one of the models, they're saying nasty things about me…"

"Nasty things? *Envious* things?"

"Things like, 'Look at her, the stuck-up princess!'"

There was a pause, then Dad's voice softened. "Naomi, my dear, your mother and I have told you before, unfortunately these comments will probably never go away. You must rise above them, because they come from jealous minds. You *are* a princess. It's an inescapable fact and you must simply let people take you as they find you and say whatever they want, without you taking it to heart."

I sighed. This conversation was still not going at all as I wanted. Maybe if I mentioned the other thing that had made me so uneasy.

"But I'm worried that Elise only chose me because I'm a princess, Dad. You see, when she first asked me to be her model, she made a great thing about *not* having chosen me because I'm a princess, and said she'd picked me because of my straight back and things like that. But why did she say anything about being a princess? I've just got the feeling she thinks she'll get more attention or something...and that feels...wrong to me."

There was another pause before Dad replied, slowly and gently. "I don't think you should let it worry you, Naomi. Even if she did choose you because you're a princess, think of the good that has come out of it. Think of Just Water."

Now I felt really panicky, and started gabbling away at top speed because I was so desperate for Dad to find something to disapprove of. "But you should see what I've got to wear! It's a really short, tight evening dress, and everyone'll be staring at me!"

There was silence from the other end of the phone. I held my breath. At last it seemed I'd said the right thing. My mind started racing ahead, imagining Dad calling Miss Carol and saying, "On no account can I have Naomi wearing skimpy little dresses and cavorting on a catwalk. Please tell Miss Owen that we are not allowing it!"

But then I got a shock because Dad suddenly chuckled. "I remember the first time your sister Sisi wore an evening dress. I can still picture her tottering along in high heels. I know it's hard, Naomi, but you must try to develop your Western side, while hanging on to your African roots. Why not give Sisi a call? Or Mary?"

We only talked for a minute or two after that before I hung up. I'd called for Dad's advice, but now I was almost wishing I hadn't. Maybe I ought to do as he suggested, and call one of my sisters. But I knew really that I'd never do that. There's an eight-year gap between me and Mary, and then Sisi is two years older again. They're very close to each other, but have never been close to me because of the age difference.

The phone call had definitely made me feel worse, not better. There was no way that I'd be able to back out of the show now that my dad was supporting it.

* * *

The next day I felt nervous all day because Elise had asked me to go to my first fitting. It was French last period with Mam'zelle Clemence, and I'd asked Katy not to bring up the subject of the fashion show, because I didn't want the spotlight back on me again and everyone talking about me, so now I just had to hope that Mam'zelle Clemence wouldn't bring it up herself. Penny was in my French class and I'd already seen her whispering to another girl, but I'd told myself not to get neurotic. After all, she wasn't necessarily talking about me. All the same, I was pleased when the bell went for the end of class.

"Right, pack away zee books, girls," Mam'zelle Clemence instructed us in her lovely strong French accent. Then she broke into a big smile and called across the classroom, "I 'ear you 'ave 'ad your arm tweested, Naomi! Fantasteeeek! Only twelve years old and already bound for zee catwalk!"

I could have died, but I quickly latched on to something she'd said, to show Penny I wasn't showing off about it. "You're right, Mam'zelle Clemence! I did have to have my arm twisted and I'm going to be really nervous with everyone watching me. I bet I'll be useless at walking like a model."

"No, no, no! You weel be lovely!"

"Why did you agree to it, if you hate it so much?" came Penny's clear voice, cutting through the chatter and the noises of bag-packing.

"I...I..."

"Because it's for a good cause," said Katy, defending me.

"What?" said Penny.

"It's a charity called Just Water. I..." How could I explain my involvement with the charity without sounding arrogant? "I've always supported it."

"Excellent!" said Mam'zelle Clemence, beaming. "Eet is all verrrrry exciting! And now, Katy, we 'ave our own fashion club, yes?"

Katy nodded. She didn't need reminding. Fashion club with Mam'zelle Clemence is her favorite time of the whole week.

As soon as we were outside and out of earshot of anyone, Katy turned to me. "Don't worry, Naomi. It's only Penny who's got a problem. You mustn't let it get to you."

"But she thinks I'm a show-off and she's spreading it," I moaned. "I'll feel terrible if everyone starts thinking bad things about me."

"They won't. I was talking to some girls from Beech House yesterday and they were really happy for you. In fact one of them said she could totally see why you'd been chosen, and she wished she looked like you!"

"Seems like word's gotten around pretty quickly." I sighed.

I was rather disappointed to be missing debate club today, but as it was the first time Elise had asked me to go for a fitting I thought it might seem rude to say I couldn't come. Mia had promised to report back about what was debated, so at least I wouldn't feel that I'd completely missed out.

Katy suddenly frowned. "Oh, I wish I didn't have to miss your first fitting, Naomi, but we're customizing belts in fashion club today, which will be really fun, I know. You will tell me all about it later, though, won't you?"

"Of course I will," I reassured her, taking a deep breath to calm my nerves. "See you at dinner."

As I went off to the design room, I did feel a little bit better because of what Katy had said about the girls from Beech House. I told myself that gradually everyone would get used to the idea of a sixth grader being one of the models, and then hopefully they'd stop talking about it. And anyway, I only had to walk down the catwalk three teeny little times and that would be that. Finished!

But somehow I still couldn't stop my heart from beating faster at the thought of entering that strange world where I didn't fit in.

The busy atmosphere in the design room was exactly the same as the last time, except that there seemed to be more models around. Lara was fitting a layered skirt on a very beautiful girl.

"That's Petra," said Elise, when I still couldn't take my eyes off her a few moments later. "She modeled last year. She'd look good in an old shopping bag with a piece of string for a belt!" Elise's eyes glinted with something I couldn't quite understand.

"She looks stunning in that skirt and top!" I said enthusiastically.

"What, you like that grungy look? Quite honestly, Naomi, anyone can achieve that kind of design." I was shocked that Elise had spoken in such a hard tone. But a moment later her voice turned light and bright. "Wait till you see your finished prom dress! I don't want anyone pinching my ideas so we'll stand behind this screen... Okay, strip right down."

I was relieved that I didn't have to take my clothes off in full view of everyone. Petra didn't seem to mind standing out in the open, but I would have felt totally uncomfortable. When I'd agreed to be Elise's model, I'd never even considered how often I'd have to get changed in front of people. I hoped there'd be screens on the night of the show, otherwise I knew I'd feel young and stupid compared to all the ninth and tenth graders.

Elise unwrapped the dress from some tissue paper and slipped it over my head. "You just stay still. I'll get it into the right position."

It felt nice and smooth on the top half, but then it pinched my waist and seemed too big for my hips. The bottom of the skirt was very tight, with a slit up the back. "That's so you can walk!" said Elise, smiling. "Looking good, Naomi! Looking good!"

"Are you going to take it in a little around here?" I asked, pressing the material to show how much spare there was sticking out from my hips.

"Don't do that!" said Elise.

"Oh, sorry!" I felt terrible.

"That's the design. It's supposed to exaggerate the female shape. That's why I've used such a stiff fabric, obviously. I might give you an extra inch around the waistline, though. Lift up your arms."

I did as I was told while she fiddled with the waist. "Do you have any silver stilettos?" she went on.

I shook my head. I didn't have stilettos of any color.

She grabbed a big tapestry bag and pulled out a pair of high heels. "I'll get you silver ones for the show, but try these on for now."

I'd never worn such high heels and I felt really wobbly. "I'm not sure I'll be able to walk in these…"

"Which is why we have such things as practices and rehearsals!" laughed Elise. "Now let me look at you." She stood back. "You'll be wearing really long white fishnet gloves with silver and gold trimming, and this will be the last of my six outfits to be shown, so I want it to be the most stunning of all. I'm thinking that on your head you could wear… well, we'll see about that later."

I hoped she didn't want to change my actual hairstyle, because I always wear it in cornrows and I don't like anything different. "Um…you won't do anything drastic, will you?"

"No, no, no. I won't alter your hair at all. I'll probably just add…something…"

Elise was being rather mysterious, but at least I didn't have to worry about my hair.

"Okay, you can take a look in the mirror if you want. I'll bring the free-standing one over here, then no one else will see you."

When I saw myself I actually gasped. I looked so different. I turned around slowly and looked over my shoulder. I really didn't know what to think. It was all so strange.

"Like it?"

I did the smallest of nods, and then felt that I probably ought to be a bit more complimentary. "You're really talented to have designed all this."

She waved her hand dismissively. "Oh, that's nothing. Anyway, you can get changed now. Be very careful, though. *Very.*"

I did as I was told and when I came out from behind the screen I stared in amazement. Petra was standing on a table. Another layer, which consisted of millions of colored patches, had been added to the skirt. Her top was completely plain white, which went well with her olive skin. The whole outfit looked amazing.

"Do you think that's the 'Dress to Impress for Less' category?" I whispered to Elise. "Or the 'Caj with a Dash'?"

"I've no idea," said Elise, waving at a girl who'd just come in. "Here's Charlotte. She's another designer. Hey, Charley!"

The girl strolled over and broke into a broad grin when she saw me. "Nice one, Elise. I feel honored to be standing on the same piece of floor!"

I didn't know what she was talking about, but it must have been a private joke, because Elise threw her head back and laughed loudly.

Then, as other girls came over to see what was so funny, I crept away. At the door I turned around to see that everyone in the room seemed to have gathered around Elise and Charlotte, except for Lara, who was still in a world of her own, frowning at the bottom of the skirt and pinning the hem. Petra looked completely bored and I caught her rolling her eyes and looking at her watch, as if to say, *How much longer do I have to stand here?*

I heard a few snickers and giggles coming from Elise's group of friends, and then my heart missed a beat as Charlotte's words came floating over loud and clear. "Look at Lara working away! Obviously thinks she'll be the winner!"

Immediately there came a loud "Ssh!" from Elise, as her eyes flicked over in my direction just before I left the room. I was suddenly desperate to get out into the open and see the sky and the trees and feel cold air on my skin, and I broke into the fastest possible walk down the corridor. The design room had stifled me. So the fashion show *was* a competition. There was no way I could have gotten the wrong idea *this* time. Had Elise been deliberately hiding that fact from me? And if so, why?

"Naomi!"

I looked up to see Katy waving at me and running over. "Was it good?" she called as she got closer. Then, puffing up to me, "Tell me everything! I command you!"

"Well…"

"Uh-oh!"

"What?"

"I can already tell you didn't enjoy it!"

I sighed. "You're right. I hated taking my clothes off, but much worse than that – guess what – the fashion show *is* actually a competition!"

Katy looked shocked. "*Is* it? Mam'zelle Clemence never mentioned that. How do you know?"

"I heard one of the designers saying something about Lara working hard because she thought she would be the winner."

"Oh!" Katy's eyes widened and she gave me an anxious look. "But I'm sure that's nothing for you to worry about, Naomi. It'll only be the designers who are being judged."

"But why did Elise lie to me, Kates?"

Katy frowned. "She shouldn't have, should she? But maybe…she thought you'd get yourself in a state about it and it was better for you not to know."

I didn't answer because I wasn't at all sure about that.

"I wish I'd been there with you, Naomi." Katy linked her arm through mine. "Actually, I didn't think you'd be finished yet. I was just going down to Pets' Place to see Buddy. Do you want to come?" She switched to a gabble. "Or were you going to the secret garden, because I don't mind if you were? We can talk after."

That's what I really like about Katy, the way she's so caring and thoughtful the whole time. "No, I'll come and see Buddy with you. We can talk on the way."

Buddy is Katy's rabbit. He lives in Pets' Place during school, with Mia's guinea pigs, Porgy and Bess, and various other pets. Katy really loves Buddy. I love animals too, but I've never had any pets because Mom and Dad won't allow it. They don't think animals belong in people's houses and I've always just accepted that.

"So, come on, tell me all about the fitting," said Katy, sounding excited again.

"Well, I was allowed to get changed behind a screen, thank goodness, and the top of the dress is nice but then it sticks way out on my hips and it's really narrow at the bottom, with a slit up the back. And you should see the high heels – I felt like I was on stilts! I have no idea how I'm going to walk a single step."

"I can't wait to see it. I bet you look fantastic! Were there lots of people there? Did you see any of the other designs? What did you see? Come on!" Katy's eyes were dancing. She really did want every detail.

"Lara's model, Petra, was there. She's so beautiful, and I looked at the outfit she was wearing and wished like crazy that we could trade. It was a gorgeous flared skirt with lots of patches, and a plain white top. You'll love it too, when you see it. It's just the kind of thing *you'd* design."

We'd reached Pets' Place by then, and Katy took Buddy out of his run on the grass and cuddled him while we went on talking about my fitting.

"Elise made it really obvious she wasn't particularly impressed with Lara's outfit, Kates."

"Seems like she's the jealous type, doesn't it – one of these people who just has to be the best all the time."

I nodded. Katy was right. After that we went on talking as we went over to dinner, but it was mostly about fashion club. Then Mia joined us and filled me in on debate club. I couldn't concentrate though, because those words that Katy had said wouldn't leave me alone. She was right. Elise does seem to have to be the best. It's obvious from the way she tries to hide her outfits so no one can steal her designs, and also from that hard look in her eyes when she was criticizing Lara's "grungy" designs. The truth is that Elise isn't a very nice person, certainly not the kind of person to want to try and protect me from feeling anxious about the competition. So just why had she tried to keep me in the dark? Could it be that she thought she stood a better chance of winning if she had a princess for a model, and she guessed how much I'd hate the thought of that, so she decided to pretend there wasn't a competition?

I was still confused though. Surely she didn't think she could keep it from me forever?

No, probably just until I was so deep into fittings that it was too late to pull out.

Chapter Four

Elise had asked me to come for my next fitting at three o'clock on Saturday afternoon. I wasn't looking forward to it one little bit, because I couldn't stop thinking about the way she'd deceived me. Katy kept saying that Elise couldn't possibly have thought that she'd do better in the competition just because of having a princess for one of her models, but I think that was Katy's way of trying to keep me from feeling anxious.

"Don't think about it any more, Naomi. You're getting yourself into a state for no reason. Remember, it's all for a good cause!"

I made myself take her advice, and tried to relax.

Katy and I were right on time arriving at the design room, so it was a surprise to find no one there except Lara. She was working at one of the special sewing machines in the corner of the room, and didn't stop when we went in. She couldn't have heard us.

"Hi," I said quietly.

She looked up with a start. "Oh, you made me jump! I wonder what planet I was on just then." She laughed, then looked around. "I don't know where Elise is. I've been the only one here for ages."

"I like this fabric," said Katy, eyeing what Lara had on her machine.

"Me too. It's pretty, isn't it?" said Lara enthusiastically. "This is for the 'Prom' category. My other model, Sophie, is going to wear it, but I'm worried that it won't be ready in time because there are so many sequins to sew on and it's full-length." She finished off what she was doing and snipped the thread, then gently took it out from the machine and held it up.

"It's beautiful!" I breathed. "You're so talented, Lara!"

Katy's eyes were bright. "I love the asymmetric line of the skirt. It's so much more original than a fishtail." I thought she was talking about the kind of dress that went in at the back of the legs, then fanned out again, but I wasn't sure.

"What color sequins are you going to use?" Katy asked.

"I was thinking blue but I'm not sure. Maybe a mixture of colors."

"Blue would look great." Katy had a dreamy look in her eyes, and I knew she'd be trying to imagine the finished outfit. "How much of it are you going to cover with sequins?"

"Well, at first I thought the whole thing from the waist down, but now I'm not so sure."

"I can imagine a big swathe of them right across here," said Katy, spreading her fingers wide and slowly sweeping her hand from top to bottom in a diagonal line just above the material.

"Hmm," said Lara, frowning. She handed the dress to me. "Can you hold it up for me, Naomi?"

I did as I was told and Lara and Katy stood back to get a different perspective. "Do you know, I think you're right." Lara smiled and nodded slowly. "Yes, that would look great!"

Katy's face lit up and it was such a dreamy magicky moment, but then it got broken a second later as the door crashed open and Elise came rushing in. "Sorry, guys. Lost track of the time." She stopped in her tracks when she saw me holding the dress and her eyes narrowed. "What are you doing with my model, Lara?"

Her voice was light but there was something in her tone that made me shiver. Lara didn't reply. She just quietly said, "Thanks, Naomi," as she took the dress from me and sat back down at the machine. Then, as Katy and I dutifully followed Elise over to the other side of the room, Lara called, "And thanks for the idea, Katy!"

As I was getting changed behind the screen I heard Elise ask Katy in a low voice, "What idea was that?"

"Oh nothing much," Katy replied. "Just something to do with sequins."

"Sequins aren't going to make up for the lack of a fishtail," said Elise. "They're the thing these days. Wait till you see Tansy's dress." Then she turned to me. "Okay, I've only got ten minutes before Tansy's fitting. Here. This is the jacket for the casual outfit. You can put it on over that top you're wearing."

It was very crisp, in a dark red with black braid around the edges. The sleeves were short and the collar was also short and stuck straight up.

"There'll be one big button and you'll undo that when you get to the end of the catwalk, just before you turn."

I was starting to hate the word "catwalk." It felt like a punch in the stomach.

"Yes, that looks fine. I want to see about the accessories for the prom dress, so take the jacket off." She handed me a pair of long fishnet gloves. "Remember I told you you'd be wearing these?"

I looked at Katy when I'd managed to roll and wiggle the gloves up my arms, but I couldn't tell what she was thinking. Personally I felt really silly, but that was probably just me.

"Good," said Elise, nodding. "Now this choker..." She was clasping a gold ruffly thing around my neck. "And you'll have gold earrings... You see, the whole look is about mixing gold and silver and I want the top and bottom silver, hence the silver shoes. Here, put these on again for now." She pulled the high heels out of her bag.

"So is there going to be something silver on Naomi's head?" Katy asked, a little hesitantly.

Elise's eyes seemed to flicker, but then settled into a look of pity, as though Katy's question was really pathetic. But actually it was exactly what I'd been wondering.

The answer was rapped out briskly. "Yes. A pair of silver barrettes." She patted my arm. "You'll look great! Hey, Tansy!"

We all looked over to see Tansy approaching. "Hey! How's it all going?" she asked brightly.

"I was just telling Naomi about the silver barrettes she's going to be wearing," said Elise.

Tansy grinned. "Sounds cute!" Then she pouted, pretending to be upset. "Do I get to wear anything on my head, Elise?"

"No, but you might be wearing a gag over your mouth!" Elise laughed, tapping her friend gently on the arm.

Tansy roared with laughter, then started to peel her clothes off. "Okay, let's get on with it!"

I quickly disappeared behind the screen and took off the gloves and choker, and put my sweatshirt back on. When I came out, Katy had gone back over to Lara, while Elise was pretending to tell Tansy off. "Stand still! You're such a fidget. You should take a page out of Naomi's book, Tanz!"

"Yes, but I've never been trained!" said Tansy in a fake whine. "I'm not used to standing around regally while people look at me."

I felt my hackles rising as I handed the accessories to Elise and walked off.

"Bye, Naomi!" she called after me. "See you here again tomorrow, about eleven, okay?"

"Actually, I'm going on the ice-dance outing tomorrow, so I won't be able to make it." I knew I sounded more stressed than I'd meant to, but it felt good to be turning her down. I just hated the things Tansy was saying. It was as though the two of them were in a little private club and they actually wanted me to feel awkward because of what I am. It's all right for Dad to say that I just have to accept it and let people take me as they find me, but I can't do that. I just can't.

"I heard what Tansy said, by the way," said Katy, as we walked back to Hazeldean. "Don't take any notice, Naomi."

I stopped walking and blurted out what I felt. "But I hate it. It's as though I'm one big joke to them."

"Poor Naomi... But it can only get better from now on. I've watched tons of behind-the-scenes programs about the fashion industry, and everyone's always frantically panicking that they won't get their designs finished in time for the big show. It'll be like a hive of industry in that design room, and no one will have time for talking about anything except their designs, I swear."

As usual, Katy had made me feel a little better, and when she suggested we went down to the track for a run, it seemed like a perfect idea. "No need to get changed is there?"

I agreed, because we were both in sneakers and track pants. There weren't many people there, but we spotted Grace running around the track long before she spotted us, and Jess was at the other end of the field with her precious camera. She was staring up at the tall oak trees with their solid gnarled trunks.

"Let's run over and see what photos she's taken," I suggested.

So that's what we did, and Grace came sprinting in the same direction as soon as she spotted us. We all got to Jess at the same time, even though Grace had much further to come.

"Is it my imagination or are you getting faster, Grace?" asked Katy, laughing and panting.

"I'm trying to speed up my warm-up," she replied, frowning at her stopwatch.

"You mean that was only the warm-up?" I spluttered.

A group of sixth graders nearby laughed and came

over to join us. "It's really depressing on the track when Grace is around," joked a girl named Sabrina. Then she turned to me. "Hey, how's the modeling going? What do you have to wear, Naomi?"

I didn't really feel like talking about it, but these were nice girls and, after all, they were only showing an interest.

"Well the evening dress I tried on is so scary, I'm not sure I'll actually make it down the catwalk without falling over!" I said, which made everyone burst out laughing.

"You're so lucky, you know!" said a girl named Robyn, looking envious. "I'd love to have been chosen, but obviously they don't normally choose sixth graders, do they? It's just with you being a princess and everything."

"No, it's not because of that," I quickly pointed out, feeling myself getting worked up again. "It's because..." But I trailed off. I didn't want to start thinking these kinds of thoughts again just when I was trying to relax about the whole thing.

"...because she's got the right shape and stance," said Katy firmly. Then she turned to Grace. "What were you saying about your warm-up? Do you want me to time you?"

I knew Katy was deliberately getting everyone

off the subject of the fashion show for my sake and I felt grateful. But even though we'd stopped talking about it, I couldn't keep it from filling up my mind until I thought my head would burst.

Chapter Five

As the show drew nearer, I grew more nervous than ever, but the good thing was that Katy turned out to be right. Nothing more was said that made me feel awkward about being a princess, because the designers only talked about their clothes. From what Katy had described, I'd imagined them working their fingers to the bone, but the only one who seemed to be doing any hard work was Lara. The others just did a lot of walking around and looking at everyone else's designs.

I heard quite a few of the models complaining that it wasn't fair they were only allowed to model for one designer. Tansy said it was stupid that she had to go to all the rehearsals for the sake of three little turns on the catwalk. But Lara explained to Katy and me that the teachers were concerned that people would be spending too much time at fittings if they were modeling more than three outfits.

Katy usually came with me to fittings and she really enjoyed going around and chatting with all the designers and asking them what they were doing. I loved having her there, too.

"Lara is easily the nicest," she said to me one time. "She talks to me as though I'm her equal, whereas the others treat me like I don't understand anything about fashion design, and that really makes me mad."

"It would get to me as well," I admitted, feeling sorry for her.

"Elise is the worst of them all," she added. "If you weren't modeling for her, I wouldn't go anywhere near her. I hate the way she's secretive about her collection, yet goes around being really critical of other people's stuff."

I knew what Katy meant. Elise definitely wasn't my favorite person and, if I was honest, I felt awkward in all the clothes I'd tried on so far. For the "Caj with a Dash" category I had to wear something that was so formal I felt like I was going for an interview. Underneath the red jacket there was a fitted shirt with no collar, and then on the bottom half I had to wear a pair of tight, cut-off pants and some little ankle boots. Katy said I looked great, and I had to admit it was amazing that Elise was able to design and make clothes like these, but I couldn't help it, I just didn't feel comfortable wearing them.

"Never mind, perhaps you'll get to wear something you like more in the 'Dress to Impress for Less' category," Katy said, trying to cheer me up.

But when I asked Elise about it, she told me to chill a bit. "I haven't finished that outfit yet. You can't hurry these things, Naomi. Creativity is a slow process. I don't know what Lara's trying to prove, working away like a crazy person."

I hated it when Elise said things like that, because I really liked Lara, and I also admired the way she worked so hard. She'd customized some of her clothes by adding buttons and patches and beads to make something stunning out of something ordinary, and Katy and I both loved that way of working.

Quite a few of Elise's friends turned up to look at her outfits and they all said how lucky I was to be what they called "the chosen one."

"Imagine! Only a sixth grader! Makes me feel

positively ancient. Clearly we're all past it, girls, as far as modeling is concerned!" said one girl, pouting theatrically, which made everyone laugh.

I didn't laugh though. I just stood there in my ridiculous clothes, gazing longingly at Lara's collection, and feeling nervous because I had to face a new terror soon. The dreaded full rehearsal.

The night before the rehearsal, I told Katy and the others my fears. "I'm going to stick out like a sore thumb!" I wailed. "Elise showed me how to walk, kind of strutting along, all wiggly hips and funny high steps. I'll never be able to do it!"

"Yes you will!" said Georgie. "Come on, let's have a little mini Amethyst rehearsal."

But I knew I'd be far too embarrassed. "There's no room in here."

"We can go in the hallway just outside. No one ever comes up to this floor besides from Miss Jennings."

"Leave the poor girl alone," said Katy, putting her arm around me. But Georgie was already heading purposefully out of the dorm with Mia and the others behind, so Katy and I just found ourselves following like sheep.

"Do you know what music you're having?" asked Mia.

"No, I don't know anything!" I said, feeling panicky.

"Well, it'll be something loud," said Katy, "and it'll be the perfect speed for walking so you can keep in time with it as you walk."

The more we talked about it, the more scared I felt. "Oh no, I'll never manage that!"

"I can give you a little tip if you like," said Mia quietly. "The music will pretty likely fall into sections of eight beats, so if you get used to counting to yourself in eights, you'll have much more of a feel for when you've got to start and when you've got to turn and everything."

"Oh thanks, Mia," I told her warmly. "I need all the advice I can get."

"Okay then, watch me!" said Georgie. "You've got to swing your hips."

"Okay, Georgie," said Katy, "if you're the demonstrator, try to place each foot in front of the other one, as though you're stepping on a straight line."

Georgie set off down the hallway, while the rest of us all joined in clicking our fingers at the speed that Mia set up. I was quite impressed. Georgie looked totally model-like.

"Oh I so wish it was you and not me!" I told her

when she'd gone up and down a few times, grinning at all of us, and turning around with a really cool swing.

"It's true, Georgie is great," said Katy, looking thoughtful.

"Hey, thanks!" said Georgie, winking at Katy.

"No, seriously," went on Katy, "the reason you look cool is because you're confident. You're good at showing off, and that's what all models do."

"So you're calling me a show-off!" said Georgie, pretending to be offended.

"Okay, do you want to try, Naomi?" asked Katy.

I sighed and slumped. "I'm going to be useless, aren't I, because I can't even try it in front of my friends."

"Well if it helps at all, I wouldn't dare either," said Grace.

"Me neither," Mia agreed, shuddering.

"And I'd just be awful," said Jess.

In the end the others said they'd go back into the dorm so there'd only be Katy with me, and finally I plucked up the courage to walk once along the corridor.

"Wow! That was brilliant!" said Katy. "You're a natural, Naomi, honestly!"

But I was sure she was just trying to raise my

spirits. "I don't feel like a natural. I feel like an idiot."

"Do it again and walk in time with my click, and just lift your head a little."

I did as I was told because it was easier the second time.

"I tell you, Naomi, you look amazing, and that's just in track pants and a top!"

The third time I tried it I actually felt pretty comfortable with myself, because Katy's words had given me confidence. She insisted I showed the others, so they all came tumbling out of the dorm and stood there waiting for me to do my thing, which felt much more daunting than when I'd done it for just Katy.

I took a deep breath and started immediately before I could change my mind. I just took a few steps in one direction then paused, before turning as confidently as I could, and after another pause I went back the other way. When I stopped I felt a hot wave of embarrassment creeping up my back, but then I got a nice surprise because they all started clapping, and Georgie whooped so loudly that Miss Jennings appeared.

"I recognize that loud voice!" she said, giving Georgie a strict look.

"Sorry, Miss Jennings," said Georgie. "But I think you might have been a touch whoopy too, if you'd seen the way Naomi struts her stuff!"

I saw Miss Jennings hide a smile. She's very strict, but Georgie always wins her over. I was just dreading the thought that she might ask me to demonstrate, but she was obviously busy because she disappeared in a hurry, thank goodness. I had a couple more tries, to get used to the audience, and then we all went to get ready for bed.

Maybe it won't be as bad as I think, I told myself as I brushed my teeth. But I was shivering in my jammies. It was one thing doing it for my close friends, but a whole other thing doing it in front of a bunch of ninth and tenth graders and teachers at the full rehearsal. I closed my eyes and thought about Abina. Tomorrow morning I would get up at seven o'clock. Abina would get up at five, and spend the next six hours collecting dirty water in order for herself and her family to survive. And the saddest thought of all – they might not.

I opened my eyes and looked hard at myself in the mirror, feeling something strong gathering inside me.

You will be nervous, Naomi, but that's a small price to pay.

Walking into the main school hall where we have assemblies, I couldn't believe how it had been transformed. I stood and stared from the back, feeling like a complete impostor and wishing I could go and hide.

Think about Abina.

Elise appeared from behind me and I was relieved to be able to talk to someone.

"It's incredible, isn't it?" I began. "I mean it really looks like a catwalk…"

"Oh this is nothing!" laughed Elise. "This is just for the first rehearsal to give us an idea of layout, so the models know how long the catwalk is. Wait till you see how they decorate the place for the actual show, and then there'll be all the lights too. It'll be stunning. For today, you're simply getting used to the music. No one gets changed or anything. It's called a walk-through."

I was relieved we were taking it one step at a time. Seeing how many people were involved with something that sounded as simple as a walk-through was really scary, though. There were two teachers, and I recognized one of them because she'd directed a play that Georgie was in before Christmas. "Oh, there's Miss Pritchard!"

"Yes, she's the choreographer," said Elise.

"Choreographer! We don't have to dance, do we?" I asked, feeling rising panic for about the tenth time.

Elise must have found me hysterically amusing. "Hey, Tanz!" she called to her friend, who was standing around at the front with all the other designers and models. "Naomi thought you had to dance!"

I felt mortified, because lots of people turned around, grinning and snickering.

"Come on, we're starting!" said Elise, putting a hand on my back and pushing me forward.

The other teacher was directing some of the models and designers to stand on one side of the stage, and some on the other.

Elise was marching on ahead of me now, but Lara was by my side, explaining things to me in a low voice. "On the night of the show you'll all get changed in the wings, and the curtains will be closed, apart from a gap in the middle that you go through at the start of your walk."

I nodded, feeling grateful for every bit of information I could possibly get about this big scary event.

"I guess they'll keep the curtains wide open for today," she went on, "so you can all watch each other and get used to the choreography."

That was such a scary word. I wished it wouldn't keep coming up. "What exactly do you mean by choreography?"

"It's just the number of steps you take and the order you walk in, that's all."

I thanked Lara, then went to join Elise. She'd plonked herself right near the middle of the stage with Tansy. Standing beside her, I felt horribly conspicuous. Quite a few of the designers were used to me being in the design room, but some of the models hadn't seen me around before. They were exchanging looks with each other and whispering behind their hands, and I wished I could magically fast-forward to the next rehearsal so everyone would be used to me and no one would give me a second glance.

It was going to be awful when we had to actually get changed in the wings. I know some people don't care at all about that kind of thing, but I do. Maybe we'd be allowed to find a little private place somewhere. Lara was just behind me and I decided to ask her, because I wasn't going to risk Elise broadcasting my silly question to the whole auditorium.

"Do the models *have* to get changed in the wings?" I whispered.

She gave me a sympathetic smile as she nodded. "But nobody ever has time to look at anyone else, I promise you. It's completely crazy once it starts."

It was so kind of Lara to try and take away my fears. I gave her a grateful smile.

Elise was talking excitedly with Tansy when I turned back to her, but all the chatter stopped a moment later as the teacher I didn't know raised her voice.

"Okay, let's have some order, girls. I want this to run like clockwork because we only get two more rehearsals before the real thing, so listen carefully." Lara looked at me and mouthed "Miss Owen" and I nodded and smiled, grateful again that she was keeping me in the picture. Miss Owen was speaking briskly. "You may feel a little ridiculous, but I want you models to go through the motions of pretending to get changed in between your turns on the catwalk. It's important that we do this preparation today so that when we try it for real there are no surprises. Now this is the order. Listen carefully. And models, make a mental note of who you're following so we can roll it through without any glitches. It's the same order for all three categories. The first time, Miss Pritchard will talk you through the actual catwalk part as you're walking, then at the end she'll keep back anyone who needs extra help."

I gulped, and got ready to concentrate so I wouldn't forget who I was following, even though the name probably wouldn't mean anything to me and I'd have to ask Elise which girl it was. Miss Owen explained that it was the "Caj with a Dash" category first, followed by the "Dress to Impress for Less," and lastly the "Prom" category. I was to follow a girl named Emily, who was following Petra, so that was a relief because at least I knew who Petra was. It turned out Emily was modeling for Charley, and I recognized her by sight.

Next, Miss Pritchard took over the instructions. "Now you might feel a little exposed today, because we're having the curtains pulled all the way back so everyone can watch each other, and also so that Miss Owen and I can get a full picture of what's happening backstage as well as on the catwalk. You'll have to concentrate hard, please, and don't talk when you're pretending to get changed. It'll be silent backstage on the night, so let's get used to that today. Those of you who've never done a fashion show before can learn from those who have. Kelsey, can you demonstrate the counts, please."

My heart beat faster as pounding music suddenly exploded into the hall and Miss Pritchard counted loudly and rhythmically above the music, while Kelsey did the most perfect demonstration.

"One – two – three – four – five – six – seven – eight – two – more – stop – two – turn – two – stop – two – walk – two – three – four – five – six – seven – eight."

I was so happy that Mia had mentioned the counting in eights and I'd been practicing counting to eight whenever I was walking on my own. The music stopped and Miss Pritchard's voice sailed effortlessly around the hall. "Okay, I hope you all got that. You walk for eight beats, until you feel the end of the musical phrase, then the next set of eight consists of two more steps, a pause for beats three and four, turn for five and six, and pause again for seven and eight. Then the third set of eight is the return walk."

Kelsey had to demonstrate twice and I watched her really carefully, and thought I had it by the end of her second turn.

"Now," went on Miss Pritchard, "Tasha, you must make sure you are counting Kelsey's third set of eight and set off immediately after they are finished, so that your first steps overlap with Kelsey's exit. On the night, I'll be standing backstage to cue you, but once you're out there, you're on your own. So let's watch Kelsey one more time, everyone, particularly the way she walks. See how she strides out and also notice that she's got a very natural swing to her hips, but she's placing her feet one directly in front of the other, as though she's walking along a line that's been painted on the floor. I also want you to notice how Tasha and she overlap. Sarah, you can follow right after Tasha and so on… Okay, everybody clear?"

I swallowed. I thought I was clear about what I was *supposed* to do, but I had no idea whether I *could* do it. Also, I was scared stiff that I was going to look awful and be the only one kept back at the end for not getting it right.

The music started again and every part of my body tensed up. I was almost the last one on Miss Owen's list, and as girl after girl swanned up and down the catwalk, I grew so nervous I felt sick. Not everyone got the counts totally right, but all the girls looked incredibly grown-up, the way they pushed their hips forward and wore pouty looks on their faces. Katy and the others were obviously just being kind when they said I was good. I didn't look anything like this when I walked.

My heart was in my throat by the time Petra set off. Then I stepped forward, like I'd seen the others doing, as soon as Emily set off, and finally, I don't know how my shaky legs allowed me to take a single step, but somehow I found myself on the catwalk. I remembered Katy telling me to hold my head up, but apart from thinking about that, my whole brain was taken up with getting the counts right. I managed to turn smoothly, but felt like dying when Miss Pritchard stopped counting after my first eight steps and just stared at me. She'd been counting non-stop up till that point. How embarrassing. I was definitely going to have to stay behind. And no wonder. It would completely spoil the fashion show to have someone so much younger among all the older girls. She was probably going to order Elise to choose a different model from ninth or tenth grade.

"Great job!" Elise whispered, when I came back into the models' waiting area. But she was hardly looking at me, so I knew she didn't really mean it. "Now pretend you're getting changed," she went on. I felt stupid miming taking off a jacket, but that's what everyone was doing all around me, so I just did it. I kept telling myself that it didn't matter if Miss Pritchard or Miss Owen threw me out of the show. Although it would be embarrassing, they'd be doing me a big favor because I wouldn't have to worry and get nervous any more.

The music went on and on until all thirty models had had a turn on the catwalk. Then it faded and stopped, and finally the place erupted in excited chatter, but Miss Owen soon put a stop to that.

"Pretty good for a first time, girls. Nice work! Now on the night, there'll be a pause of about five minutes here, and then we'll plunge straight on with the next category, which will have different music but exactly the same counts. Some of you went wrong with the counts last time, but I think most of you realized when you'd made a mistake, so let's try it once more for practice, pretending we've moved on to the 'Dress to Impress for Less' category."

Miss Pritchard took over then, and said that most people had managed the actual style of the walk really well, and it was largely a question of confidence. "Let yourselves go! You have to show off, girls, and make people want to look at you." My heart sped up a little because I was dreading her mentioning the names of the people who hadn't gotten it right and needed to stay behind. "On the other hand," she went on, "several of you *over*did it, and looked awkward and false." She paused and her eyes ran over us all. "Naomi…"

My stomach clenched at the sound of my name, and I was aware of lots of eyes on me.

"Where are you, Naomi?" Miss Pritchard was trying to see over the heads.

"She's here!" said Elise loudly.

"Yes, Naomi, you've got a very natural poise and elegance. But you look anxious. Just let yourself go, dear, and you can turn that poise into something great." She turned instantly away from me and spoke to everyone else, while I stood there shaking. "There are quite a few others, too, who need to relax and just go with the flow of the music. But as I said, some of you went the other way, and overdid the swing of the hips. Now I don't want to curb your enthusiasm, but you need to tone it down a bit. Naomi's an example of someone who's used to being in the public eye, which is probably why she looks so poised. Try and find the happy balance, girls."

Miss Pritchard stopped talking then, thank goodness, because I hated her praising me and talking about me being in the public eye. What must all these experienced models who'd been in last year's fashion show be thinking? It only took a few seconds for me to find out because I distinctly heard one of them whisper sarcastically, "Great! Even Miss Pritchard sucks up to her just because she's a princess."

A few moments later, as Miss Pritchard talked in more detail about how your arms and head and hips should be positioned, I took a subtle look around me, and noticed that everyone seemed to be listening very carefully. That was a big relief. At least no one was aiming evil looks in my direction. But now I just wanted to get on with the rest of the rehearsal and then flee from this hall to my secret garden.

Finally, after two more run-throughs, Miss Owen decided that we'd done enough for a first rehearsal, and she read out the names of the girls on her list who needed to stay behind. There were only a few and I wasn't one of them.

"Are we allowed to go?" I whispered to Lara.

"Yes, it's hot in here, isn't it? I can't wait to get out. Great job, by the way. Don't worry about jealousy. It goes with the territory. Just keep your head down and get on with it, like I do." She grinned at me and I thanked her with my eyes for being so sweet, then crept toward the door.

It wasn't till I actually opened it and was almost out in the hallway that I heard someone say, "Hey, looks like you were right about your little prodigy, Elise!"

And then Elise's voice rang out for all to hear.

"I know! I am *so* going to win this competition. I told you, girls, it wasn't for nothing I found myself a princess! Even Miss P commented on that natural do-it-for-the-cameras thing she's got going for herself. And wait till you see her in a tiara. Stroke of genius, eh?"

"I know!" squeaked Tansy. "That's such a fantastic idea!"

My hand stayed on the door handle and my head crowded with raging thoughts. First Elise had lied about the competition, then she'd lied about the silver barrettes, and now I knew for sure about the worst lie of all – she really *had* chosen me because I'm a princess. I wasn't leaving this auditorium now. My blood boiled.

Abina, you don't need me to stick myself in the limelight. I'll still make sure Just Water *helps you, but I'm pulling out of this ridiculous fashion show. Right now.*

Chapter Six

I let go of the door handle and turned to face the room, my back against the door, my heart racing with anger. Everyone was buzzing with excitement. No one was paying any attention to me. Miss Owen had a crowd of girls around her, who all seemed to be talking at once. Miss Pritchard had put the music back on at a lower volume and was walking down the catwalk with exaggerated rhythm, a girl on either side of her. All three were counting loudly.

Still I just stood there like a statue, and the more I took in the scene before me, the more I hated everything about it. Katy might love this world of fashion, but it wasn't for me. A few people were turning to leave, chatting and laughing, coming toward the door where I stood. Elise was one of them. I watched the bright smile quiver around her mouth as her eyes changed from sparkling to puzzled when she noticed me standing there, tense and still. She knew something was wrong. And one by one the others stopped talking and stared.

"What's up?" asked Elise, suspicion narrowing her eyes.

My determination hadn't left me. I was still angry. "I'm not doing it."

It was as though my words had punctured the buzz and the throb of excitement in the hall, and it was seeping out of our small solemn corner.

"Of course you are! Don't be silly!" snapped Elise.

Her friends' eyes widened as they jerked their gazes from me to Elise and back again.

"I'm not being silly. Now I know you picked me because I'm a princess, I can't do it. You even lied to me about what I'd have on my head. A tiara is going to make me look stupid." There was an expression I wanted to use. I'd heard my sister use it once. I searched for the words and they popped into my head. "You're just playing on my royal status."

There was another silence, then Elise's face softened. "Oh, don't take any notice of me. I didn't mean it…"

The top layer of my anger was fading now and embarrassment was starting to creep up my back and my neck. I was still determined to stick to my guns though. "Sorry, Elise. You'll have to find someone else. I feel completely out of place here, and I felt even worse on the catwalk."

Then suddenly everyone was speaking.

"Naomi, you looked great!"

"Miss Pritchard even singled you out for praise!"

"You fit in perfectly!"

Then Elise's voice, with a hard edge, cut in. "Anyway, it's too late. You're committed now."

A horrible guilt was making my throat hurt and I thought I might be about to cry. That would be awful. I knew I mustn't be swayed. I had to stick to my decision. It felt right. It *was* right. "Sorry, Elise," I repeated. "It's…I mean, I'm sure it's not too late for you to find someone else."

Elise raised her voice. Her eyes glinted furiously. "What? Someone exactly the same size and shape as you? Yeah, right!"

I quickly pulled open the door and rushed out before I could change my mind. Then I ran along the hallway, feeling the tears gathering behind my eyes, and when I got outside the cold air hit me, but I didn't care. It was better than the sickly hot air in the auditorium. Still I ran and ran, with tears dripping down my face. I passed a few people, but they were hunched against the cold and huddled together, not paying attention to me. I gave them a wide berth and kept my head down until I was on the track, where I finally slowed my pace and wiped my face on my sleeve. It was too cold to walk though, so I started running again and didn't stop till I reached the secret garden.

Going through the gap in the hedge, I waited for the usual feeling of peace to come over me. But it didn't. I sat down on the bench and bunched my knees up, hugging them tight. I stayed curled up like this, with miserable thoughts raging inside my head, until I felt like a block of ice.

What had I done? How could I have been so dramatic? I usually think about things carefully before I act, but I'd just walked away from the whole show without any consideration for poor Elise. *Poor* Elise. No. That wasn't true. She'd lied to me. And anyway, there were masses of girls who were more or less the same size and shape as me, who'd fall over themselves to be her model. It was true that she might have to do a few small alterations to her outfits, but nothing much. And an older girl would look ten times better than me in those designs. I hadn't even tried on the third outfit yet, so there wouldn't be any alterations to that one.

All the same it was true that I'd acted like a prima donna, and I couldn't help feeling embarrassed about suddenly announcing that I couldn't go on and dramatically running away. The more I thought about it, the more uncomfortable I felt. I started to imagine myself telling Katy and the others what I'd done. It wouldn't be easy to explain, and I wasn't at all sure how they'd react.

Inside my skirt pocket my phone vibrated. I pulled it out and looked at the number. The screen said *Home*. Mom occasionally called at this time, just before dinner. So now I was going to have to explain to Mom what had happened as well, and I simply wasn't prepared. But I couldn't *not* answer her, so I pressed the green button.

"Hi, Mom." And I suddenly realized that the fashion show didn't have to be mentioned at all if I could keep the conversation on other things. My brain started scouring around for what I could talk about, but Mom didn't give me time to say anything.

"Just a quick call, Naomi. I wanted to let you know that Miss Carol called to ask our permission for you to be interviewed by someone from the local television station on the night of the fashion show, and of course we were delighted because it's all good publicity. So you might like to start thinking about what you're going to say. You know how your father always says it's much better to be prepared."

My heart had been sinking more and more as Mom had been talking. I was going to have to admit what I'd done. I couldn't pretend nothing had happened, because eventually my parents would find out and it would make things worse if they discovered I'd been keeping it secret. But I'd play it down. Yes, that's what I'd do.

"The thing is, Mom, we had the first rehearsal just now and it was obvious I didn't really fit in, so…Elise is going to try and get someone older instead…"

There was silence on the other end of the phone.

I plunged on. "I'm not upset or anything…and it doesn't mean…I can't do the interview." I wasn't sure if that was true, but I was trying not to annoy Mom too much.

"What do you mean, you didn't fit in?"

"Well…I felt too young."

"Ah! *You* felt too young. It wasn't that Elise or any members of staff thought you were too young?"

Now the silence was at my end of the phone. I couldn't lie. There was no way out of this one.

"No," I whispered.

"Oh, Naomi, tell me what happened."

Mom's voice was filled with disappointment, but I couldn't tell whether it was the kind of disappointment that's close to sympathy, or the kind that could easily tip over into annoyance. I didn't want her to be upset with me, but it's always been so hard to make her understand how I feel about being a princess and wanting that part of my life to be separate from school, and not to get in the way of how people look at me.

"Well...Elise was really boasting about how she'd deliberately chosen a princess for a model because that was sure to make her the winner of the competition, and I've got to wear a tiara, and I couldn't bear it. *And...*" I broke into another gabble. "...I can't tell you what it's like walking down a catwalk. Miss Pritchard said you have to show off, and you know I hate people looking at me. I just wish I'd never agreed in the first place, but the others thought I ought to, and all I could think was how it would be helping Just Water, so that's why I said yes."

I heard Mom sighing heavily. "I'm sorry, Naomi, but as you say, you shouldn't have agreed to it in the first place. I know Elise has acted badly, but two wrongs don't make a right. I can't imagine Elise was too happy with you dropping out at the last minute?"

"Um…well, there are tons of other people who are my size who'd love to be her model…"

"All the same, if she's fitted clothes to your exact measurements, she's sure to have to make alterations. But more to the point, you've let her down, Naomi."

I wanted to say, "Yes, but *she* let *me* down." Only there was no point. I'd never get Mom to see that being chosen because of being a princess is unbearable for me. So I stayed quiet.

"Well I can't make you do the show, but I have to say it's unlikely you'll be interviewed as an ordinary student who has nothing to do with the fashion show. And that would be a good publicity opportunity for Just Water missed."

"I'll try and explain to Miss Owen and Miss Carol about why I pulled out, and…" I trailed off because I couldn't be sure that the teachers would understand my decision. But I hoped against hope that Miss

Carol would. She's such a fair and understanding person and I really like her.

"Think about it, and try to see things from all points of view, Naomi."

"Okay. I'd better go now, Mom. It's dinner time. But I'll...call you when I've talked to Miss Carol."

After I'd hung up, I realized I was so cold my teeth were starting to chatter, and I did a big involuntary shudder, partly because of the cold and partly because I was upset. I had tears in my eyes as I got up to go back to school.

By the time I reached the cafeteria, I was looking forward to getting some warm food inside me, but I definitely wasn't looking forward to telling the others what had happened. And I was positively dreading seeing Elise or any of her friends. In fact, it might have spread all around the ninth and tenth grade that Naomi Okanta was a selfish little prima donna, and they might all hate me. I shivered and went to join the line.

When I finally found the courage to look around, I saw Katy, Georgie and Mia waving excitedly at me. Georgie was mouthing something, because she'd never be heard above the noise of chatter and silverware on plates even if she shouted. I shrugged and smiled to show I didn't know what she was saying, though it was obvious really. They all wanted to know how I'd done at the rehearsal. I swallowed and tried to prepare some words.

Sitting down next to Katy, I started to feel ridiculously nervous. But I kept telling myself she's my best friend and is sure to support my decision. I wasn't so confident about Georgie, but Mia would probably make her understand how I felt.

"So, tell us all about it," said Katy immediately.

I swallowed and blinked. "Well, it was awful, actually..."

All three of them gasped.

"Why? What happened?" asked Georgie, stopping eating and staring at me, wide-eyed with curiosity.

I took a deep breath. "I hated it. I felt so nervous. My legs turned to jello—"

"But did you walk the way you showed us at Hazeldean?" Georgie interrupted.

"I did my best..."

"And did you manage to fit your steps to the music okay?" asked Mia.

"Yes..."

"Well you must have been great!" said Katy. "I bet you're just being modest."

"I felt so young..."

Katy put her arm around me. "I hope no one criticized you or anything just because you're the youngest."

"What did Elise say?" asked Georgie.

"What did the teachers say?" asked Mia. "Weren't they impressed with you?"

This conversation wasn't going at all as I'd hoped. By now I should have made my big confession and the others should all be offering me bags and bags of sympathy.

"Well, Miss Pritchard—"

"Miss Pritchard!" interrupted Georgie. "Oh, you mean you've got my total heroine in charge of the fashion show?"

"She's in charge of the choreography. Miss Owen's in charge of the whole thing."

"Don't keep interrupting, Georgie," said Katy. "What did Miss Pritchard say, Naomi?" Her eyes were full of concern again.

"Um…she said I was doing it really naturally…" I knew I'd have to mention that, because if my friends heard it from someone else they'd be upset that I hadn't said anything about it. But at least I could convince them that this was the most embarrassing part of all. "…And she said the reason I looked natural was because I was used to being in front of cameras. Everyone must have thought I was a big show-off. I mean, I actually heard someone say that Miss Pritchard was sucking up to me because I'm a princess..."

Katy's eyes gleamed darkly. "Just ignore the horrible person who said that about you being a princess. At least it was only one person. There wasn't anyone else, was there?"

"Well, no...but I hated it!" I quickly reminded them all.

"I know what you mean, Naomi," said Mia. "I'd have hated it."

I felt grateful to Mia, but her little comment did nothing to stop my heart from hammering as I started to build up to my big confession. "And Elise was really showing off about me and – you'll never guess – she actually admitted she'd only chosen me because I'm a princess and she thought that would make her win!" My voice sounded strange and high, even to me.

"That must have been horrible to hear," said Mia quietly.

The others all nodded gravely, but I'd really been hoping they might go nuts and say it was an unforgivable thing that Elise had done, and maybe one of them might even say I ought to quit.

But nobody spoke, so I went on in my squeaky voice. "And guess what else, Kates, she even lied about the silver barrettes in my hair. I heard her telling her friends I was going to be wearing a tiara!"

There was another small silence and I looked at their wondering faces, feeling my confidence dissolving.

"Well she definitely shouldn't have been so deceitful about the tiara," said Katy, wearing a big frown.

"That was completely out of line!" Georgie agreed.

Yes, keep going...

"But then she probably guessed you'd hate the idea of wearing it," Katy went on.

"At the end of the day it's only a fashion accessory though, isn't it?" said Georgie. "It doesn't mean anything, Naomi, honestly."

My confidence took a plunge then, because although everyone agreed Elise had behaved badly, nobody thought it was *that* bad. And what Katy said next made me really panic at the thought of having to make my admission.

"The other stuff Elise said is ridiculous, though! I mean, she'd never win just because one of her models is a princess! The judges are grown-ups, aren't they? They'll only be interested in the designs.

They won't even know you're a princess. Who *are* the judges anyway?"

"I...I don't know actually." I felt the last grains of confidence slipping through my fingers. Katy had said something amazingly obvious and incredibly true. And what I had to say next was going to sound so pathetic. It had to be said though.

"Anyway, you know how I can't bear people liking me for what I am and not for what I'm like..."

Georgie sat up straight as she took a slow breath and her eyes filled with suspicion. "What...have... you...done...Naomi?"

"I...I...told Elise I wasn't going to be in the show." I looked down and braced myself.

"Not going to be in it!" squeaked Georgie. "What? The whole show? You've said you're not going to be a model, you mean?"

I nodded helplessly.

"You're nuts!" Georgie pursed her lips in disapproval and slumped her shoulders dramatically.

Katy shook her head slowly, as if she was imagining the scene. "Whoa! Elise must have gone ballistic!" Then her eyes flickered and she spoke hesitantly. "Don't you think...you're kind of... committed, after all this time?"

Mia looked down and I guessed she agreed with that.

"Elise isn't exactly...happy," I stammered. "But... I'm sorry, I have to stick to my principles." I sighed and repeated, "Sorry," with a crack in my voice.

"Poor old Naomi," said Mia. "You have to follow your feelings, though."

That little comment of Mia's gave me the tiniest ray of hope that my friends would understand why I'd done what I'd done.

Katy frowned. "Yes, you're right, Mia," she said, nodding. A little sigh of disappointment escaped her and I knew she'd be thinking about how she was going to miss the design room.

I put on my most positive tone as a small shred of confidence came back to me. "You could still go along to the design room."

"I might feel a little out of place," said Katy. She had been staring thoughtfully at the table, but she suddenly sat up straight and smiled brightly. "Don't worry about me, though. The important thing is that you've done the right thing, Naomi. You've stuck to your principles."

Mia nodded.

I looked at Georgie. Somehow I needed all my friends to approve of what I'd done, because that might help to take away some of the guilt and embarrassment I was still feeling.

Georgie wrinkled her nose. "I don't expect Elise'll have any trouble finding someone else, so...don't worry about it, Naomi."

I was so relieved I wanted to cry. There were only Grace and Jess left to tell now, and they weren't half so absorbed in the fashion show as the other three.

Katy took her arm away but gave me a sweet smile. "Your food's getting cold. It's delish by the way!"

I realized I was starving, and was about to dive in when I happened to glance up and see Elise marching across the cafeteria in my direction. My fork dropped to my plate with a clatter and the hand holding my knife trembled. What had happened today wasn't going to go away in a hurry.

If ever.

Chapter Seven

My stomach felt knotted, especially as Katy and the other two had definitely spotted Elise, and it was clear that she was on her way over to me. The weird thing was that as she got closer her face began to change, and by the time she'd reached our table she was wreathed in smiles.

"Naomi, hi," she began, squashing herself on the bench between me and Katy. "Listen, sorry about earlier. I've been thinking about how you must feel and I just wanted to kind of reassure you that there's nothing to worry about. I mean, I realize you hate all the princess talk and I promise you, from now on, the 'P' word is banned! Taboo!" She grinned as she made a gesture slashing the air with the side of her hand.

Now my stomach felt even more knotted, because it was obvious Elise was here to persuade me to change my mind about the show, and I didn't know what to do. I so badly wanted to do the right thing, but I needed time to think it through properly and I longed to talk to my dad too.

Elise suddenly swiveled around so she was addressing her next words to Katy and the others as well. "Anyway, the main reason I wanted to talk to you is because I never told you about my dad, did I?"

I shook my head, wondering what on earth she could be about to say. And it seemed such a coincidence when I'd only just been thinking about my own dad.

"Well, I deliberately didn't mention this before because I didn't want you to get excited and act any different from usual..." Her eyes were all sparkly, and it wasn't just the glittery eye makeup she was wearing.

I waited silently, but Georgie was too curious to keep quiet.

"So, yeah...what about your dad? Why would

Naomi be excited? Is he a talent spotter or something?"

"Well, you've practically hit the nail on the head!" said Elise, looking mysterious. "My dad is very big in Topshop. He goes around to lots of fashion shows – I mean seriously important ones, all over the country, and overseas too. And every so often he spots someone who he just knows is going to hit the big time and be a supermodel..." Elise paused, as though to let her words sink in. Georgie sat up straight, looking totally impressed, and I felt myself shrinking in my seat. "Anyway, the thing is," went on Elise, fixing me with a serious but excited look, "I told him about you..." She seemed to freeze for a moment. Maybe she saw the panic all over my face. "I mean, I didn't tell him you were a princess... No way!" She started to gesture with her hands, and her voice grew louder. "I told him how you're a natural on the catwalk and everything, and he wants to take a look at you at the fashion show, because, get this..." I felt a heaviness settling in my stomach where all the knots had been just a few moments before. "...He thinks you could be the second Naomi Campbell!"

"Naomi Campbell!" screeched Georgie. "She's the biggest supermodel of all time, isn't she?"

If Elise was hoping this would persuade me to come back into the fashion show, she couldn't have said anything worse. Mia and Katy were both looking at me anxiously. They knew me well. Even Georgie was biting her lip now.

"I'm sorry," I began quietly. "I should never have said yes to you in the first place. It's all my fault, but I was so happy about the money going to Just Water that I got a little carried away. The thing is, I hate the limelight…"

The twinkle had completely left Elise's eyes and I saw her lips going into a thin line. "So that's it, is it?"

I nodded.

"Right." She stood up quickly and flung me a horrible look. "Thanks for wasting my time."

"Sorry."

"Sorry isn't good enough. I'll make sure you *are* sorry, Naomi Okanta! I've bent over backwards for you, getting Miss Owen to choose your precious Just Water. Other students put forward suggestions too, you know. Well, maybe she'll switch to one of those, so that it's at least a charity chosen by someone actually taking part." Elise's voice was growing more and more sarcastic and mocking. "She's not going to be too impressed when I tell her that Miss Pritchard's little prodigy has decided she doesn't want to join in after all!"

I felt myself cringing from the mean look in her eyes before she turned and stomped off. A few seconds later her words sank in fully.

"Oh no!" I said in a panic. "What if she does manage to get Miss Owen to change her mind about Just Water?"

"She won't!" said Katy. "It's on all the posters, remember?"

She was right. Posters advertising the event had gone up on lots of the school noticeboards.

"Yes, but you saw how angry she was. And Miss Owen will probably be really upset with me too."

Georgie gave me an apologetic look. "Are you sure you've made the right decision, Naomi?"

Despite everything, it was easy to answer her, especially now I'd really seen Elise's true colors. "Yes. I just made the decision too late."

My one huge worry was the threat to Just Water, though, and I knew I must go and see Miss Owen as soon as possible. But first I had to see my dorm mom, Miss Carol. I wanted to explain my side of the story before she heard it from someone else. But I needed her help too. Houseparents are the closest thing to real parents that we students have at Silver Spires, and I was desperately hoping that Miss Carol would understand and support my decision.

When I told Katy where I was going, she immediately offered to come with me.

"I'll be okay thanks, Kates," I said. "See you at study hour."

All the way to Hazeldean I planned what to say to Miss Carol, but the more I searched for the right words, the more worried I felt. How was I ever going to make her see why I'd pulled out of the fashion show at this late stage?

I knocked on the door of her apartment, which is on the ground floor at Hazeldean, and prayed that she'd be in. It was really important to tell my side of the story before she got to hear about what had happened from Miss Owen.

"Come in."

She was working on her computer.

"I'm sorry to disturb you…"

"That's all right, Naomi." She smiled, taking her glasses off and moving over to sit in an armchair. "Come and take a seat. What can I do for you?"

My heart was racing as I sank into her nice cozy armchair. If only I was here to curl up and watch TV, instead of having to explain the impossible.

"You know the fashion show?" I began quietly.

"Uh-huh." Miss Carol's face didn't show any sign of suspicion that I was about to break some bad news.

"Well…" I only paused for a second, then it all came tumbling out. "I've told Elise I can't be her model… You see, she was boasting today that she only picked me because I'm a princess and that was sure to make her the winner. She was talking about the tiara I've got to wear, which she'd never mentioned before. She didn't know I was listening, you see. She thought I'd gone out. But I hadn't, and I got upset and said I wanted to quit. And I know I've let her down, but I just didn't think she'd been honest with me. Only now I'm really worried, because she's furious and says she's going to get Miss Owen to change the charity to a different one, and I don't want Just Water to lose out."

Finally I stopped. Miss Carol's face was very still and grave. She didn't speak at first, and it was tempting to cram a few more words in, but I knew I'd said enough – probably too much in fact – and I had to keep quiet and wait.

"Hmmm," she finally said. "Difficult one."

I nodded. "I'm really sorry, only—"

"You had the first rehearsal today, didn't you?"

"Yes."

"And how did it go apart from what Elise said?"

"It was okay…" I was beginning to get that same uncomfortable feeling I'd had when I'd started to tell Katy and the others at dinner.

"So you managed the catwalk all right?"

I nodded.

"So, it's literally that you're not happy that Elise appears to have chosen you because you're a princess?"

"Yes…" How could I make Miss Carol realize I wasn't just being petty? Maybe I hadn't made myself clear enough. "I can't bear being in the limelight just because of being a princess," I said, leaning forward. "I hate it."

Miss Carol seemed to be choosing her words carefully. "Think of Miss Owen and Miss Pritchard, Naomi. They've invested a great deal of time and work into the organization of the fashion show. Whoever Elise finds to replace you will have missed that first all-important rehearsal, and that's going to make the teachers' jobs harder."

"I know." I sighed on the inside and wished Miss Carol would say something to make my biggest worry go away. "But what about Just Water? What if Miss Owen changes the charity?"

"I'm sure you don't have to worry about that," came the brisk reply. "I'll talk to Miss Owen." She slowed down. "But I want you to think about continuing as a model. The question, Naomi, is this…" She gave me a sorrowful smile. "Can you let your principle go on this occasion, in order not to let people down?"

I looked at her and dug deep in my brain for the answer to that. But I couldn't find it.

"Think carefully. And come and see me any time."

"And you will remember to speak to Miss Owen, won't you?"

She nodded and stood up, as if to tell me it was time for me to go. I didn't want to go when there was this uncomfortable feeling in the air all around us, but I had no choice.

There was nothing more to say.

I didn't do very well with my assignments during study hour because I couldn't concentrate properly. My mind was going over and over the conversation I'd had with Miss Carol. Afterward, up in the dorm, Georgie filled Grace and Jess in on what had happened earlier, then everyone wanted to know what Miss Carol had said to me. I told them as much as I could without actually saying the one question that I hadn't been able to get out of my head ever since Miss Carol had asked it. *Can you let your principle go on this occasion, in order not to let people down?*

The trouble was if I said it out loud there was a chance that they might all think I ought to let go of my principle. And then what would I do? It was all so confusing and I was close to tears.

Katy must have realized, because she put her arm around me. "Don't worry, Naomi. No one's going to think badly of you."

I nodded but felt too sad to speak. It was kind of Katy to say what she said, but I didn't believe it for a second. The truth was that no one would have any sympathy for the girl who let everyone down at the last minute. I felt overcome with frustration and sadness. When I manage to do something well, people say that the teachers are sucking up to me because I'm a princess, and when I pull out so people *won't* think that, everyone thinks I'm being a stuck-up prima donna.

I can't win.

Chapter Eight

The next few days were the worst since I'd joined Silver Spires last September. I dreaded seeing Elise around school. Luckily she was hardly ever in the cafeteria at the same time as me for meals, but some of the older students were definitely talking about me. I knew I wasn't imagining it. I would glance around and catch sight of people whispering behind their hands, their eyes flicking away when they saw me looking.

Miss Carol left it a while and then asked me if I'd given any more thought to rejoining the fashion show. She'd caught me on my way in from running club. I was with Grace and Katy, and they went on up to the dorm to get changed while I followed Miss

Carol into her apartment, feeling hot and anxious as I stumbled out my all-important question.

"Have you...did you...get to ask Miss Owen whether she's still going to have Just Water as the charity for the money raised?"

"Yes," said Miss Carol, sighing. She pursed her lips a little and gave me a long, careful look as we both sat down. "I must say, Miss Owen isn't particularly pleased that you've let Elise down at the last minute, but I tried to explain your side of the story as best I could." She didn't smile and I felt as though I was being told off. "You don't need to worry that she'll change the charity, Naomi, but the media might not be interested in interviewing you if you're not involved with the show. As Miss Owen pointed out, it's great that you're involved with the charity, but you're not helping it by letting this publicity opportunity slip."

I nodded and felt uncomfortable. Miss Carol still hadn't smiled.

"I take it you've not changed your mind?" she asked quietly.

It was such a big question. If only I could explain to Miss Carol that I'd been arguing with myself non-stop since the last time I'd seen her, that I didn't know what to do, that my brain felt like one big dilemma with thoughts bumping round and round, then round and round again…

I've always said I don't want to be liked just because I'm a princess.

But Elise said it was for my straight back, and even Miss Pritchard said I had poise…

No, Elise only chose you because you're a princess, and she lied to you about that.

Yes, I'm glad I've pulled out. It was the right thing to do.

But what about Just Water? You might not get interviewed.

The money will still go to them…

But you've turned your back on them. You're no longer involved with the event that's raising money for them.

But I can't do it. I've got to stick to my principles.

Can't you let it go, so you won't let people down?

I won't be letting people down. Elise will find someone else.

The teachers aren't happy.

Miss Carol coughed, and I realized I'd not answered her question. She was looking at me carefully. What should I say? I couldn't think any more.

I did the smallest shake of my head, feeling terrible. "Sorry." Then I thanked her for trying to stick up for me to Miss Owen, and left her apartment, sad that she hadn't given me a real smile on the way out, and went along to the common room to see if Katy and the others were there.

I never did go inside though, because something stopped me in my tracks when I was on the point of pushing the door open. It hadn't been closed properly and I clearly heard my name mentioned. My heart started banging, and I knew I shouldn't be eavesdropping like this, but I just had to find out what was being said about me. The next person to speak was Penny.

"It's ridiculous!" she was saying. "No wonder everyone's annoyed with her."

"I know, and all because she doesn't want to wear a tiara!" That was someone named Fay.

"It's pathetic," another girl said, and I heard lots of indignant noises of agreement. "I mean, a tiara is just a fashion accessory. Lots of people wear them, not just princesses."

"Exactly. She ought to stop thinking about herself for a change, and think about other people!"

I was raging inside. Half of me wanted to go crashing into that common room and get it into these girls' heads that it's *not* just about a stupid little tiara. But the other half was holding back, because in my heart of hearts I was starting to wonder whether they were actually right, so I crept away sadly to the secret garden.

My mind was in too much turmoil to sit still on the bench in the secret garden, so I decided to walk around instead. It didn't matter where. Anywhere would do. I was desperately trying to work something out. I had to be sure I'd done the right thing, because I was even starting to doubt myself now that *everyone* seemed to think I was in the wrong. *Was* I just being selfish? Did Katy and my other close friends really think that as well, but were too kind to say it?

Miss Carol's question was still pounding away in my head, like loud music that I didn't want to listen to. *Can you let your principle go in order not to let people down?* Impulsively, I pulled out my cell phone and called home. I needed another chance to get Mom to agree with my point of view.

But it wasn't Mom who answered. It was Dad, and I felt myself getting tongue-tied as I spoke about my confusion.

"Mom probably told you... Did she say why? I mean, why I'm not...?"

"I was expecting an important call, Naomi, so I'll be brief..." Oh dear, I'd caught Dad at completely the wrong moment. "Naomi, your mother said you'd call back when you'd spoken to Miss Carol. We've been wondering what she said."

Dad was clearly in a hurry, coming to the point as briskly as this. Miss Carol's words rang in my ears and I blurted them out to Dad almost before I'd realized it. "She asked me if I could let my principle go this once so as not to let people down."

There was such a long pause after I'd spoken that I wondered if I'd lost reception. "Dad?"

"Yes...yes. I think you should take note of what Miss Carol said, Naomi. She's absolutely right... I've always taught you that our principles are important, but it's true that sometimes, if it's for the good of other people, we need to let go of them momentarily. I know you'll make the right decision. I'm relying on you. And very much looking forward to seeing you on the catwalk."

I didn't answer, but my head buzzed with confusion, and it was still buzzing as I hung up a moment later when Dad said he had to free the line for his important call. I stood perfectly still, rooted to the spot. I had to try and figure this out. Dad was relying on me. This was an impossible situation. What on earth was I going to do?

I started thinking through all that had happened

leading up to that first full rehearsal. I went over those times I'd been in the design room when I'd felt left out of the tenth grade club because I'd not understood what they'd all been laughing about. It made me cringe with embarrassment to think how naïve I'd been not to get that I was the target of their jokes.

"Nice one, Elise. I feel honored to be standing on the same piece of floor." Charley had roared her head off, and I hadn't realized what she'd meant about me being a princess.

"Do I get to wear anything on my head, Elise?"

"No, but you might be wearing a gag over your mouth!"

How could I have been so stupid as to not realize that they were talking about the tiara I was going to have to wear.

Then I pictured the big rehearsal itself. And when I got to the part where Elise told her friends laughingly that she'd deliberately picked a princess so she'd be sure to win the competition, I grew angry all over again, and knew my principles were just too important to let go. Just Water would get the money. I might be losing one publicity opportunity, but I could make up for that during the Easter break. Yes, I would work and work and make up for everything during the break. That's what I would do. But for now, even if no one in the world understood how I felt, I wasn't going to be messed around and toyed with. I had to stand by my feelings.

My walk hadn't made me feel any better though, because now I knew that Dad totally agreed with Miss Carol, I felt more awful than ever. I set off back across the track, thinking I might as well go straight to dinner. I was already late. On the way, I quickly went to the bathroom near the cafeteria. Lara was in there. She had her back to me, drying her hands under the electric dryer.

"Hi!" I said nervously. I wasn't sure what Lara thought of me now.

She turned and smiled when she saw it was me. "Oh hi."

And that was when I noticed she'd been crying.

"Oh, Lara, what's the matter?" I couldn't help asking. But immediately I realized I shouldn't have said anything, because it was obvious she was trying to hide it. "Sorry, it's none of my business..." I pushed open the door to one of the stalls.

But when I came out again she was still there, texting really quickly. I washed my hands and a second later our eyes met in the mirror and I saw she had tears rolling down her cheeks. This time I had to find out what was the matter, because I couldn't just leave her in this state.

"Is...there...anything I can do?"

She wiped her eyes. "It's all a disaster really."

"Wh...what?"

"Well, Elise has taken my model, Petra."

I gasped. "What do you mean, taken her?"

"Kind of lured her away from me with big promises of stardom when Petra gets spotted by Elise's dad. It turns out he's some kind of talent spotter."

I couldn't believe what I was hearing. "That's exactly what she said to *me* to try and persuade me to change my mind and be her model still."

Lara laughed a dry little laugh. "But you weren't interested?"

I shook my head.

Then she suddenly drew a deep slow breath. "I know I'm being silly. These things happen. I'm just going to have to pull myself together and get someone else."

It suddenly hit me that it was all my fault that Lara was in this terrible position.

"Oh Lara, I'm really sorry. It's totally because of me that you're having to find someone else. I feel awful."

"Don't worry. I don't blame you for not wanting to model for someone like Elise. She and Petra are the selfish ones, not you."

An enormous wave of relief swept over me. Lara understood me. "You mean…you don't think I was wrong to quit when I heard Elise saying she'd gotten herself a princess so she was sure to win?"

"Of course I don't. And to tell the truth I was relieved when I heard what you'd said to Elise. It's not that I wanted Elise to be in a tight spot or anything, it was just that I knew how she'd make you suffer if she didn't win the contest, when she thought she had a winning card with you being a princess. You see, the thing about Elise is that she has to be the best, and when she isn't the best, she makes sure everyone thinks it's someone else's fault."

I felt myself shuddering at the thought of my narrow escape, but that wasn't helping poor Lara. Her phone suddenly bleeped and she glanced at the text. "My mom's replied." She smiled at the screen. "She's so sweet. I just told her what happened and listen to what she says…" Lara started reading. *"Sometimes these things are meant to be. Who knows, your replacement model might turn out to be even better!"*

"She sounds like a great mom."

"Yes, she's cool. Anyway…" Lara glanced at

herself in the mirror. "I don't look like I've been crying, do I?"

I shook my head. "Not at all."

"Okay, I'm off to find myself a wonderful replacement. Wish me luck!"

At dinner I told Katy and the others what I'd heard the girls in the common room saying, and then all about the conversation I'd just had with Lara. They listened wide-eyed and open-mouthed, only interrupting to tell me that the girls in the common room were silly and jealous.

Then when I'd finished, Mia and Grace spoke at exactly the same time. "Oh, poor Lara!"

"How horrible is that Petra girl?" said Georgie, wrinkling her nose in disgust.

"But Elise shouldn't have gone to Petra in the first place, should she?" said Jess.

"It's because she was one of the models for the winning designer last year," I said a bit flatly. Then I recalled the look in Elise's eyes when I'd said how beautiful Petra was in the design room. I realized now that Elise had been eaten up with jealousy that Petra was modeling for Lara and not for her. Well, she'd gotten her wish now.

"What's the matter, Katy?" asked Mia.

I quickly looked up and saw that Katy was staring at me in a most peculiar way. It was as though she was holding her breath and I had to give her permission to let it out.

"What?" I asked, completely confused.

"Don't you see?"

"Don't I see what?"

Now she looked as though she was keeping a massive secret and trying to stop herself from spilling it. "*Wonderful* Lara, who we both think is *talented* and *kind* and *sweet* and utterly *cool*, with her *amazing* grungy clothes, which are *sooo* much nicer than Elise's, is..." Katy said the last four words very slowly. "...short...of...a...model."

I nodded and waited for her to go on, but she still seemed to be holding her breath, and when I looked at the others I realized they were all doing exactly the same thing. In the end it was Georgie who couldn't contain herself for another second.

"You could be *Lara's* model!" she squeaked.

"But I don't want to be a model!" I quickly protested. "That's why I dropped out. I only wanted to be involved in the first place because of Just Water..."

But even as I was gabbling away I could feel my

mind opening up to this crazy new idea. What Katy had said was right. Lara was totally different from Elise. I hadn't pulled out because I didn't want to be a model, I'd pulled out because I couldn't bear to be *Elise's* model. It would be hard finding the courage to face her, and even harder to cope with everyone staring and making comments. But I had to try. I knew that for sure now.

The others must have noticed a change in my expression.

"Yesss!" cried Georgie, as though I'd already agreed.

I shook my head as something obvious occurred to me. "No, she probably won't want me."

"Well, why don't you find out?" said Katy quietly. Her eyes were really dancing with happiness. "Go on, go now."

"The poor girl's hardly eaten a thing!" said Georgie.

So I stuffed down a few mouthfuls, then went off to find Lara.

She was in the design room working away on her own, but this time she heard the click of the door and looked up.

"I had a thought..." I began.

She didn't say anything, but her eyes never left my face.

"I mean...I'm probably too late and, anyway, I know I'm too young...and you must tell me if you've already got someone...or if you'd prefer an older model..."

She stood up and came toward me slowly. "Are you saying what I think you're saying?"

"I'm saying that...I...could be your other model... if you want..."

She broke into a massive smile, but then suddenly looked really serious. "You're not offering because you feel guilty, are you?"

"No," I quickly reassured her. Then I tried to think exactly why I was offering. "Just...because it feels like the right thing to do."

"You total star!" She gave me a tight hug, then looked at her watch and laughed. "How much can you try on in five minutes?"

I laughed too. "Not a lot. I've got to go to study hour!"

"Okay, what are you doing tomorrow at lunchtime?"

"Nothing."

"Excellent, we'll sort it all out then." She looked

as though she'd just remembered something important. "And do you have a club after school?"

I shook my head.

"Good, because that's when the second rehearsal takes place!"

I gulped and felt myself tense up at the thought of facing everyone. Lara must have seen my worried face. "There's no problem, honestly. Everyone thinks it's totally wrong of Elise to have taken Petra off me, so they'll be pleased I've found myself a replacement."

Then she patted her pocket, and I guessed her phone was in there. "Good old Mom! Right again. Some things *are* meant to be!"

That was a sweet compliment. I smiled inside and thought about Dad proudly watching me walking down the catwalk. But then the smile dissolved into a new wave of anxiety as a picture of Mom and Dad in their royal gold traditional outfits, among all the normally dressed parents, suddenly flashed through my mind. I bit my lip and squeezed my eyes tight closed. At least I wouldn't be wearing a tiara on the catwalk now, but with my parents in the crowd, no one would be able to forget that I'm a princess. I heaved a silent sigh. I so wished my parents understood how I hated all that sort of attention, but I just had to accept that they never would.

* * *

Lara met me outside the hall at the end of school the following day so we could go into the rehearsal together. We'd had a fitting at lunchtime, and luckily she'd hardly had to make any adjustments – there was just one top that needed taking in a bit. I was so relieved.

"Okay, brace yourself," she whispered as she pushed open the door. We were very punctual, so not many girls had arrived yet, thank goodness. The two teachers were there, though, and I glanced nervously at Miss Owen. She broke into a smile when she saw me.

"Oh good, you haven't left us after all, Naomi?"

"Elise and I have done a little trade," explained Lara tactfully.

Miss Owen looked slightly confused at first, but then she nodded and said, "Well that's fine. As long as every designer has two models, that's all that matters."

"And I'm glad there are no *new* models to train, just some rejigging of the order," added Miss Pritchard, as the door opened and a whole crowd of girls came in at the same time.

I saw Elise among them and quickly looked away.

"Just ignore her," said Lara, out of the corner of her mouth. "Come on, let's get into our place. Some of the models are practicing in the actual outfits because they want to make sure they can walk okay," she explained, as we went over to the stage.

"Oh no! I hadn't thought about that! I ought to make sure I can manage stilettos!"

Lara laughed. "You're forgetting who you're modeling for, Naomi. I don't do stilettos! You'll be wearing wedges for the prom dress, but flats for the other two, okay?"

I nodded hard and smiled. "*Very* okay!" I happened to look over at Elise at that moment, and saw that she was staring at me. Then I heard her say to Petra, "I don't know what she's got to grin about. She won't look anything special in the kind of stuff Lara makes." Petra didn't reply, just looked sulky and bored, as usual.

But immediately quite a few girls spoke at the same time to me, very quietly.

"Take no notice, Naomi."

"She's only jealous."

"Don't let her get to you."

"You'll look great! Lara's a fantastiç designer."

And suddenly I wasn't nervous any more. I couldn't exactly say I was comfortable, but I felt a whole lot better than before, because everyone was being so kind and not one person asked me any awkward questions about why I'd left Elise. They just seemed happy to see me back again. Even the girl who'd made the comment about Miss Pritchard sucking up to me was looking at me as though I was a human being and not a slug. It was more than I ever could have hoped for.

"Who am I supposed to follow, Lara?" I asked, in a last-minute panic.

"Louisa. See, she's that blonde girl over there."

And then, after a few words from Miss Pritchard, the music was put on and the rehearsal began.

My friends were all waiting for me outside the auditorium. "So how did it go?" they instantly wanted to know.

"I think it was okay," I said.

"That means it was fine!" said Katy, smiling. "You look so much happier, Naomi."

"Yes, I am happy now."

And I was. Except for one thing. Miss Owen had had a quiet word with me and said that she'd told the TV people that I wouldn't be available to be interviewed about the show when I'd dropped out, and she wasn't sure if they would be able to fit me in now.

"I don't know how strictly events like this are organized for TV," she'd said, "so we'll just have to play it by ear, but don't be disappointed if you don't get the interview."

I'd nodded and felt guilty again. But then I'd quickly reminded myself about working during the Easter break. And anyway, I was involved with the show again now. I felt close to my precious charity once more. And Just Water was all that mattered.

Chapter Nine

At seven twenty-five on the night of the fashion show, I stood beside Lara in the wings of the stage, feeling more nervous than I'd ever felt in my life. Five minutes to go. The auditorium was absolutely buzzing. And somewhere out there were my parents. I tried not to picture them in their regal finery – it only made me tenser than ever. I don't know who was making more noise, the audience on the other side of the heavy curtains or the designers talking urgently to their models, giving last-minute instructions about making sure we opened a jacket button as we walked, or swished a scarf over our shoulder, or swirled a skirt.

I absolutely loved what I was wearing for this first "Caj with a Dash" category. It was the plain white top and the skirt with all the very thin layers of different textures, and I felt like a bird with fantastic feathers that fanned out as I walked and wrapped themselves around me when I stood still.

My prom dress was so simple. Almost all the other designers had created dresses that were similar to the one Elise had wanted me to wear, tight-fitting and strapless, in heavy satin. Some, like the one for Tansy, were long and backless with fishtails, and others were very short. Quite a few of them had netting on the top, and all of them glittered and sparkled like crazy. Lara had made the simplest knee-length dress in aquamarine for Petra to wear. The fabric was a very fine jersey that clung to me and felt lovely and soft, and Lara said she thought the color suited me even more than it had suited Petra, which was just the best compliment.

But it was the "Dress to Impress for Less" outfit that I loved the most. Lara wanted me to wear my own jeans, but she'd decorated the pocket at the back with pink and brown Velcro strips all criss-crossed, and she'd also decorated my sneakers with the same thing. Then she'd taken a plain stone-colored T-shirt and covered it with different sorts of buttons and little triangles of colored fabric. It looked utterly fantastic.

The atmosphere backstage was electric. All the models wore loads of makeup and perfume, and the smell was overpowering. I hardly had any makeup on because Lara said I didn't need it, thank goodness. Nothing was different about my hair – it lay in its usual cornrows. But I had some special creamy moisturizer on my skin, which made it glow.

Miss Pritchard and Miss Owen were flitting around talking to everyone, and smiling with words of encouragement when model after model said, "I'm scared!"

"Nothing to be scared about!" was Miss Pritchard's answer. "You all look wonderful! Just enjoy it!"

Then Miss Owen stepped through the curtain and the audience burst into applause and cheering.

"My goodness! That's quite some welcome!" I heard Miss Owen say, which made everyone laugh. Backstage, we were too nervous to do more than smile shakily. "Welcome to the Silver Spires annual fashion show!" There was another round of applause. It was obvious that the audience was really excited. The auditorium is huge, and I knew from one or two of the designers who'd peeked through the side of the curtain that it was totally packed out.

As well as the parents of the models and designers, there were loads of students. Not everyone was interested in fashion, of course, but just about everyone in ninth and tenth grade who wasn't a model or a designer had shown up to support the event. There were lots of sixth graders too. I shivered when I thought about that. I was still getting bad vibes from some girls in my year, and that left me with a sad and frustrated feeling, because there didn't seem to be anything I could say or do to make them change their attitude toward me. It was obvious they'd only come tonight so they could talk about me behind my back.

I tried to shake those thoughts away and concentrate, because Miss Owen had finished her welcome speech and the music had started. Everyone backstage stood straight and still, and I could feel the tension around me. The show was about to begin.

I focused hard, feeling the beat of the music and trying to relax my body as I watched model after model leave the wings nervously, then stride out confidently to be met by a burst of applause. I knew I must do the same, however tense I felt.

And finally it was my turn. Walking down that catwalk was like a strange dream. I took a deep breath, and kept my eyes on the far wall as we'd all been told to, but pretended I was in the top hallway at Hazeldean, walking up and down past Amethyst dorm. I couldn't see anything because of the bright lights, and that made it easier somehow. But I could hear the audience and it was great when they clapped.

When I did the turn at the end of the catwalk, I heard a whoop and I knew it was Katy. At that moment something happened inside my head. It was as though I'd been granted permission to relax and enjoy myself and not worry about everyone watching me. I held my head high and felt my body swinging in time with the music. It was magic.

We all had to be silent backstage as we got changed, but there was lots of jostling among the designers to get to the ironing boards for last-minute smoothing out of creases. I was relieved I didn't have to worry about that. Lara's other model, Sophie, was wearing something very floaty, which was a complete contrast to my jeans and T-shirt. I really admired the way she stood completely still and looked totally calm, as Lara did up the hooks and eyes with trembly fingers.

Lara herself looked very beautiful this evening. Some of the designers had dressed up and looked practically as glamorous as their models, with hair swept up, or falling in ringlets, or straightened and sprayed. But Lara just wore her usual ponytail, her jeans, and a sparkly dark green top that she'd made herself. Elise was wearing a blue satin evening dress with an enormous bow on the back, and around her neck was the most beautiful heavy necklace of large pale-blue shiny stones.

The audience was obviously loving the show because they kept on breaking into applause and cheering, and even when they were quiet you could hear "oohs" and "aahs" from every part of the auditorium. I suppose it was no wonder. Miss Owen and Miss Pritchard and the designers had worked so hard to create something utterly glitzy and perfectly professional. And with the bright lights and the pounding music, the atmosphere was the best.

I enjoyed my second and third walks down the catwalk even more than my first one, especially when I was wearing the beautiful soft aquamarine dress. I'm sure I didn't imagine that the clapping grew louder at that moment, and walking tall and straight, I felt as though I was reaching for the moon – the same moon that Abina would see all those miles away – and I even smiled then, because I was doing this for her and it felt right.

When the last model had done the third walk, the music rolled seamlessly into another piece for the finale that we'd practiced in the last rehearsal. Some of the models had to quickly change back into outfits from the two previous categories, so that when we walked back out, in pairs and with our own designers this time, we were wearing a mishmash of outfits. I was happy because I was able to keep my aquamarine dress on. The choreography that Miss Pritchard had done was a total masterpiece, because it had been really easy to learn and yet it looked stunning. Sometimes there were only three people on the catwalk, sometimes six, and so on, up to twenty-four, and we moved smoothly in and out of shapes and patterns in our threes, stopping for several seconds so that the audience could connect up the designers with the models. The crowd didn't stop cheering and whistling and clapping from start to finish. At one point I had to pass Tansy, and she gave me the first real smile she'd ever given me. That was another great moment.

After the finale there was a fifteen-minute break while refreshments were served to the audience, and we got to sip sparkling mineral water and eat chocolates backstage, but we could only manage a thin little mint or two because we were all so nervous waiting for the judges to make their decision. I'd never seen Elise looking so tense.

"Don't talk to me, I've got a terrible headache," she said dramatically at one point.

Miss Owen asked us all to set out chairs on the stage, so that when the curtains opened for the judges' speeches we would be seated neatly with our designers. Lara squeezed Sophie's and my hands as we sat down together, then whispered to us both, "Thank you for being the bestest of the bestest models!"

Then the audience was back in its seats and the chief judge stepped onto the stage to rapturous applause. She was a very elegant lady, who really was a *lady* – Lady Alexandra Cooling. Apparently she used to be a fashion designer before she retired. Lara said she was inspirational, and I'm sure she was, but I was more interested in peering out into the audience and trying to spot Mom and Dad. The bright lights were shining full in our faces because we were still on show, so it wasn't easy to see, but I scanned every single row as far back as I could, looking for Mom's gold and white headdress with the folds of white that fell into her wrap. I was expecting to see it at any moment, or Dad's box-shaped golden headdress. But there was no sign of them. My parents simply weren't there. My heart sank, and I realized I'd been looking forward to seeing them and making them proud, ever since Dad had told me he was relying on me and looking forward to seeing me on the catwalk. Then I told myself not to be silly. They were obviously sitting further back than I could see through the glaring lights.

As the television cameras rolled, Lady Alexandra started off by saying that she couldn't understand how the standard at Silver Spires just got higher and higher every year. She praised the choreography, especially of the finale piece, and the overall organization, and then she went on to talk about the designers, going into quite a bit of detail on the three different categories, and explaining what she and the other two judges had been looking for.

"So now for the moment you've all been waiting for," she eventually said. "First I'd like to present vouchers to the two runners-up. In third place..." She paused dramatically. "Elise Finnigan-White!" Everyone cheered. "And in second place...Charley Respighi! Please come up, girls."

All eyes were on Charley and Elise as they went to get their vouchers, and I clapped and clapped along with everyone else. Elise shook Lady Alexandra's hand first, and I caught a glimpse of her face as she flounced back to her place. She didn't look at all happy and even rolled her eyes at Tansy as she sat down. Charley was smiling broadly and the audience rewarded her with an extra round of applause when she gave them a big enthusiastic wave.

"And now for our winner," said Lady Alexandra.

Beside me, Lara flinched and looked down, and I suddenly desperately wanted her to be the winner, because she so deserved it. She'd worked harder than anyone and her outfits were amazing. But a little voice at the back of my mind was reminding me that Lady Alexandra had chosen two very flamboyant designers as the runners-up, and Lara's outfits were probably just too simple.

"And so it is with great pleasure that I would like to present the first prize to..." My heart beat faster in the electric silence. "...Lara Hall!"

The sudden applause was deafening, and when Lara leaped to her feet, Sophie leaned over and gave me a big hug and kissed me on both cheeks. I clapped until my hands stung, and felt so happy for Lara. The brightest of spotlights shone on her as she shook Lady Alexandra's hand, and the two of them stayed in their smiling pose as the audience rose to its feet and camera after camera flashed and flashed, and the video camera rolled.

At last the clapping faded and the spotlights dimmed as the house lights went up. Ms. Carmichael, the principal of Silver Spires, joined Lady Alexandra on the stage and gave her a big thank you. Then everyone crowded around and congratulated Lara, and the smile never left her face. I noticed Elise didn't move out of her chair, but she sent a strong glare in my direction when she saw me looking at her. I quickly looked away and, for at least the tenth time that evening, I felt an enormous wave of relief that I'd changed to being Lara's model.

A moment later I left the stage and met Katy and the others. They were full of hugs and excitement about what an amazing evening it had been, but my eyes were continually looking over their shoulders for Mom and Dad.

"Well done, darling!"

And there was Mom right by my side, with Dad smiling behind her, and I hadn't even seen them coming over. Then I suddenly realized why. Neither of my parents was dressed in traditional African costume tonight. Both of them wore ordinary plain suits in dark colors.

Dad smiled and gave me the smallest of nods. I knew exactly what that nod meant. It was saying, *Yes, we're not wearing our traditional costume, we knew you wouldn't want it.* I felt a tightness in my throat. He knew more about my feelings than I'd thought. I introduced them to all my friends, starting with Katy, and they shook hands with each one, because that's their way. When it came to Georgie, she actually curtsied, which made Mia giggle, but it was like a magnet to the television camera. Within seconds we were being filmed.

Then Miss Owen clapped her hands to get everyone's attention and said she had an announcement to make. The chatter melted away as she began to talk about how the money raised was to go to a very important charity. My heart banged against my ribs. Miss Owen added that we didn't have a grand total yet, but she knew that Just Water in Ghana would benefit enormously from our efforts, and we were proud to be supporting such a worthwhile charity. But nobody seemed all that interested, because they all went straight back to their conversations the moment they'd dutifully clapped.

"Very pleased to meet you," said a man's voice just behind me, and I turned to see someone shaking hands with Petra, while Elise stood nearby.

"Excellent job! Well done!" he said to Petra. And I noticed she didn't look quite so sulky now. In fact she was actually smiling at him. But with his next words the smile left her face abruptly.

"I expect Elise has told you, I'm a buyer with Topshop, so I know a thing or two about clothes!" He gave Petra a friendly smile, but she flicked around to Elise and gave her a daggers look. I felt sorry for Elise's dad. How could he have known that Elise had made him out to be an important talent spotter instead of someone with the more ordinary job of buying clothes in to Topshop?

Katy and I exchanged a look, and then I realized that a man with a microphone was standing right beside me. "What does it feel like to be one of the models for the winning designer?" he asked me brightly.

I gulped and froze. What did it feel like? What was I supposed to say?

Then I got a shock, because Elise was suddenly right beside me, smiling away as though we were the best of friends. "Naomi is involved with the charity Just Water in Ghana. I actually chose the charity myself for the fashion show, because I knew how much it meant to Naomi," she went on in her loud voice. "Naomi has a big attachment to Ghana."

The man with the microphone thanked Elise,

then turned to me. "So what exactly is your connection?"

I took a deep breath.

"She's a Ghanaian princess," came Elise's bright voice beside me. She smiled right into the camera and I could tell she loved being in the limelight.

For a moment time seemed to stop, as a picture of Abina trudging to the well in the dark filled my mind. Somewhere back in the real world I heard a gasp. It sounded like Katy. She must have thought I'd be upset that Elise had made her announcement.

But I wasn't. I was actually very calm. Because I knew it was okay to use my status for a good cause.

"Is that so?" asked the man, with a new brightness in his voice.

I looked at my father to see whether he wanted to speak about Just Water, but he took a step back, and that gave me my answer.

"Yes," I said quietly to the man from the TV. "Yes, I am a princess." Then I straightened up a little. I was ready to talk now. "I spent the spring break week in my country, learning about the work that Just Water does."

I was vaguely aware that my voice seemed too strong, but then I realized it wasn't me getting louder, it was the auditorium growing quieter, and my next words were spoken into a deep silence as all eyes turned on me. I noticed Penny, surrounded by her friends, staring at me mockingly, but I didn't feel nervous. I wasn't on a catwalk now, fighting the terror of the spotlight, or even letting myself enjoy the brief feeling of rightness I'd had. I was talking about the most important thing in my life, and my voice didn't shake, because it was peaceful inside my head.

"In the north of Ghana, where the water is dirty and dangerous, there's a disease called Guinea worm. The worm grows inside you, up to a yard long, and eventually breaks through your skin." I heard the audience gasp in horror and, out of the corner of my eye, I saw Penny clap her hand to her mouth in shock. The mocking look had left her face now. I went on talking. "I've seen that sight, and I've seen the pain on the faces of the poor suffering people." I paused to let that sink in, then I continued, raising my voice slightly. "Look around you. How lucky we all are, gathered here in our beautiful clothes, not one of us more than fifty yards away from clean safe water. And now picture a girl I met named Abina. She and I are the same age. She gets up at five every morning and walks for miles to try and find water. But it's cloudy with mud, even when she's patiently waited for hours and hours in the hope that it might clear a little." I stopped and glanced around. Penny and her friends were standing completely still, wide eyes staring out of serious faces. "I want to help Abina. That's why I'm so glad I've had the chance to be involved in this fashion show. The money we raise tonight will go toward digging wells and installing pumps so that the water is no longer contaminated and the awful disease will gradually be stamped out."

Suddenly I felt exhausted, but there were four more words that needed to be said. I looked at Penny and the others as I spoke them. "I hope you understand."

Then my mom was hugging me and I was happy that I could bury my face in her shoulder and not have to face anyone for a few seconds. She was patting my back as she used to when I was a little girl, and I had to fight back tears, especially as I'd noticed Miss Carol close by, wearing such a proud look.

It was Penny's voice that made me finally look up.

"I didn't know princesses did that kind of work, Naomi. I just…didn't realize…"

I could hardly speak, I felt so choked. I'd seen something in Penny's eyes that I'd never seen before. Respect. And that meant so much to me.

"Well done," Dad said quietly, with a nod to show he approved of my speech. He didn't go in for hugs and kisses, my dad, but I could still tell how pleased he was with me.

"Excuse me, Your Majesty," said Georgie, taking a step forward and looking at Dad nervously.

He gave her a kind smile. "My dear, 'Mr. Okanta' is fine."

Georgie nodded, wide-eyed. "Um...right. I was just wondering why you didn't come in traditional costume tonight, er, Mr. Okanta?"

"Well," replied my dad, stroking his chin thoughtfully as he glanced first at Miss Carol, then at me, "sometimes we have to let go of our principles in order not to let people down."

I bit my lip and swallowed.

"Your father and I had quite a chat during the intermission, Naomi!" Miss Carol said with a twinkle in her eye. "And nice work, by the way...not just for being a great model, but simply for *being* a model. Good decision."

Katy gave me a hug. "The best!" she said.

And I hugged her back really tightly, not even

caring that the television camera was still on us. I was here with my friends and my family and I was surely the luckiest and happiest girl in the world.

*Turn the page for some
School Friends fun from Naomi!*

School Friends Fun!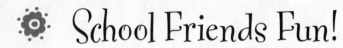

A lthough I was nervous about strutting my stuff on the catwalk, modeling in the fashion show was not only exciting, but, more importantly, it helped raise money for a great cause! There are so many ways to get involved with deserving charities and have tons of fun with your friends at the same time – here are a few ideas to inspire you!

How to make fund-raising fun!

School is a great place to hold fantastic fund-raisers, because there are lots of people to support your event. Getting your whole school involved means getting your teachers on board first, but it's worth it! Here's what to do:

★ First you need to choose your charity. Think about issues that are important to you, and do your research. Most charities will have their own website – you'll be able to find out if they're running any events you can join in with, and where you should send any money you raise.

★ If you do wear a uniform for school, have a non-school-uniform day and ask everyone to pay to wear their own clothes to school. Not only will you raise money for charity, but you'll also get a day off from wearing uniform! If you're really brave, you could even have a dress up day. Just make sure your teachers approve the idea first.

★ Hold a bring-and-buy sale! It's ideal for getting rid of your old clothes, books and CDs, while also giving you the chance to bag some bargains of your own! You could even cook up some yummy treats to sell on the day – shopping always works up an appetite.

★ Why not run a cool quiz, or even a talent contest? You can charge everyone a small entry fee to raise money, and discover your friends' weird and wonderful abilities into the bargain.
Let the entertainment begin!

So what are you waiting for? Grab your friends and have some School Friends fun!

Naomi x

Now turn the page

for a sneak preview of the next

unmissable *School Friends* story...

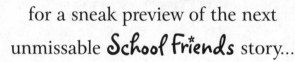

Secrets
at
Silver
Spires

Chapter One

"That's looking great, Jess."

I jumped a mile at the sound of Mr. Cary's voice because I'd been in a world of my own, blending shapes and patterns in a collage. It was my favorite class of the week: art. With my favorite teacher.

Mr. Cary and I both laughed at the way he'd given me such a shock.

"Sorry, Jess, I forget how absorbed you always get! I'll cough or something to warn you I'm approaching in the future." He leaned forward and studied my picture carefully, then took a step back and nodded to himself. "Hmm. I like the shape that's emerging through the colors of the collage."

I frowned at my picture because I didn't get what Mr. Cary meant. I hadn't intended there to be any shape.

"Look," he said, seeing the puzzled look on my face, as his finger drew a line in the air just above the painting. "It's a shoe!"

"Oh wow! So it is!"

"Let's have a look," said my best friend, Grace, coming over from her easel. "Yes, it's a sneaker!" she said, smiling to herself. "I think it's one of mine!"

I grinned at her. Some people wonder why she and I are best friends when we don't seem to have anything in common. You see, Grace is the most talented girl in sixth grade at sports and she's really good at most other subjects too, whereas I'm no good at anything except art. But Grace is a very sensitive person so she understands what it is I love about art, and when I show her stuff I've done, she doesn't just say, *Oh yes, very nice.* She asks questions and tries to see what I see. And that's great for me because, apart from Mr. Cary, Grace is the only person in my entire life who really understands me.

"Are you getting ideas for the art exhibition, Jess?" she asked me, her eyes all sparkly. Grace is from

Thailand and when she smiles she's so pretty. Her whole face kind of crinkles and lights up.

"Just what I was about to ask, Grace!" said Mr. Cary. "I'm looking forward to seeing what you come up with for the exhibition, Jess." He smiled. "Remember, you don't have to limit your work to a painting. Or even to craftwork. Last year we had sculptures, pottery, silk screening, installation art—"

"Installation art?" said Georgie, bouncing over with a paintbrush in her hand.

"Georgie, you're dripping!" said Mr. Cary, pretending to be angry, even though everyone knows that Mr. Cary never really gets upset. None of the art teachers do. That's one of the great things about art – there's no need for anyone to get upset. There's no right or wrong. No horrible words. Just wonderful pictures, and everyone simply slides into the magical world of whatever they're creating.

For me personally, I really feel the magic. I've always felt it, ever since I was four, molding a ball of play dough into an elephant at preschool. I can still remember the excitement I felt as I made two thin plate shapes for the elephant's ears. I was having a little competition with myself to see if I could make the whole elephant without tearing any pieces off the dough and sticking them back on again. I was trying to just keep molding away, teasing out the legs and the trunk and the ears and the tail until the blob of dough turned into an elephant.

Then the preschool teacher said I had to stop because it was time for a snack, and I remember how I cried and cried and stomped my foot until she promised to keep my elephant safe so I could come back to it the next day. Later, when my nanny, Julie, came to pick me up, the preschool teacher told her about me crying, but Julie didn't even ask to see the elephant, which made me sad.

After preschool, I got Julie to make play dough at home and I created a whole zoo. I arranged all the animals on newspaper spread all the way across the kitchen table, and as soon as I heard Mom's key in the front door when she got home from work – she's an accountant by the way – I rushed to the hall, grabbed her hand and pulled her through to the kitchen.

"Look!" I said proudly.

"Oooh! That's wonderful, Jess!" she said, giving me a big hug. But she hadn't looked for long enough, and I think that was the first time I realized in some funny little childish way that I could see things that some people couldn't see. I mean, I'm sure the blobs of dough looked exactly that – blobs of play dough with pieces sticking out – but to me there were all sorts of animals in there just waiting to be seen.

Then, when Dad got home – he's also an accountant by the way – he hardly even glanced at my zoo. He just patted my head and said, "Very nice. Let's put it away now, Jess."

As I got older, I realized that there are two kinds of people in the world: those who kind of connect with art (that's the only way I can describe it), and those who simply don't. So that's why I feel so lucky to have Grace. I mean, my elementary school teachers must have thought I was a good artist because they often praised me, but none of them actually wanted to *discuss* anything I'd done. Whereas Grace seems genuinely interested and says she loves trying to see the world in pictures like I do.

"I've heard that word 'installation' before," Georgie was saying. "But I don't get it. I mean an installation is like getting a washing machine or something fitted, isn't it?"

Mr. Cary chuckled, partly because Georgie had been waving her brush around while she'd been talking and had accidentally smeared green paint across her nose.

"Installation art is exactly what it says it is," said Mr. Cary. "It's all about *installing* art within its own specific environment, which might be anywhere. For example, last year," he went on, staring out of the window, "it was a piece of installation art that won first prize in the senior art exhibition. It was a birdcage hanging from a tree near Beech House, but the student had made it entirely out of natural materials and she'd left the door open to show that the bird had flown. She could have displayed the birdcage on a surface in the art room, but it wouldn't have made the same impact as it did hanging from the branch of a tree. You see, that student was making a comment about how it's not natural to keep birds in cages."

I felt my heart do the squeezing thing it does whenever I see a piece of art I love. I know I couldn't actually see the birdcage, but it was just as though I could, because there was such a clear picture of it in my head.

"That's a great idea," breathed Grace. Then we exchanged a look.

To find out what happens next, read

Secrets at Silver Spires

Ann Bryant's School Days

Who was your favorite teacher?

I had two. Mr. Perks – or Perksy as we called him –
because when I was only eleven, he let me work on
a play I was writing during class! When I was older,
my favorite teacher was Mrs. Rowe, simply because
I loved her subject (French) and she was so young
and pretty and slim and chic and it was great seeing
what new clothes she'd be wearing.

What were your best and worst classes?

My brain doesn't process history, geography or
science and I hated cooking, so those were my least
favorite subjects. But I was good at English, music,
French and PE, so I loved those. I also enjoyed art,
although I wasn't very good at it!

What was your school uniform like?

We had to wear a white shirt with a navy blue tie
and sweater, and a navy skirt, but there was actually
a wide variety of styles allowed – I was a very small

person and liked pencil-thin skirts. We all rolled them over and over at the waist!

Did you take part in after-school activities?
Well I loved just hanging out with my friends, but most of all I loved ballet and went to extra classes after school.

Did you have any pets while you were at school?
My parents weren't animal lovers so we were only allowed a goldfish! But since I had my two daughters, we've had loads – two cats, two guinea pigs, two rabbits, two hamsters and two goldfish.

What was your most embarrassing moment?
When I was eleven I had to play piano for assembly. It was April Fool's Day and the piano wouldn't work (it turned out that someone had put a book in the back). I couldn't bring myself to stand up and investigate because that would draw attention to me, so I sat there with my hands on the keys wishing to die, until a teacher came and rescued me!

To find out more about Ann Bryant visit her website: www.annbryant.co.uk